A MATTER OF MEN

BILINGUAL EDITION

A MATTER OF MEN

BILINGUAL EDITION

BENITO PASTORIZA IYODO

(CUESTIÓN DE HOMBRES)

TRANSLATION AND INTRODUCTION BY

BRADLEY WARREN DAVIS

Cover art: detail from "Las Mascaritas" by Samuel Lind
Collection of the translator
Cover photograph by Bradley Warren Davis

Translation by Bradley Warren Davis
Edition prepared by Bradley Warren Davis

ISBN: Softcover 978-1-4363-6030-2

This book was printed in the United States of America.

To order additional copies of this book, contact:
Xlibris Corporation
1-888-795-4274
www.Xlibris.com
Orders@Xlibris.com

46352

INTRODUCTION

Bradley Warren Davis

Upon entering the world of *A Matter of Men* one encounters some of the most pervasive issues regarding personal identity being faced in an increasingly complex and dysfunctional society. This collection of cinematic narratives weaves a multidimensional mosaic of manhood focusing on various aspects of identity: what it means to become a man, the challenges thrust upon the young and displaced and the responsibilities accepted or denied by adults. Each story employs a unique voice and its own point of view to illustrate how societal norms, the influence of the media, judgmental actions and stereotypes define man and his relationships. They also demonstrate how quality of life is affected by how one chooses to acquiesce or challenge these authoritative standards and benchmarks. While some stories may not resolve every issue, they inspire questions about the validity of the premise for the underlying conflict and urge exploration for possible explanations or resolutions to these dilemmas.

For more than a decade *A Matter of Men* has been entertaining and challenging readers—making them smile, squirm, laugh, whence, reflect and fidget. These works of fiction are constructed so that one could simply drink them in as a series of inventive stories, totally isolated one from the other. But this book has a broader message, which has been grasped by scholars and reviewers who recognize the thematic threads in this short, yet thought-provoking collection.

The world is changing at a rapid pace, but man's identity, sense of self-worth and acceptance of responsibility for the current state of affairs have been defined by ancient criteria, some of which were devised millennia ago. After two world wars, the twentieth century saw the advent of the United Nations, the independence of former colonies, technological innovation, the expansion of mass media, international communications, globalization, a "flat world" and increasingly democratized self-determination. With these changes, each political and societal subdivision has found it more difficult to keep its constituents insulated from the influence of other nations, religions, modern technology and secular movements. Amid this "chaos," many try to hold on to the norms of the past, especially as they relate to defining individuals, their roles and their value within the community.

This introduction will attempt to synthesize the dialogue that has emerged from critics, reviewers and scholars, while proffering observations that hopefully add another layer to the ongoing discussion. To accomplish this, we will first explore the premises behind the language employed in the translated work, followed by an exploration of some of the nuances of voice, themes, dialogue, narrative and form. The author's cinematic use of description and dialogue are also worthy of mention. Finally, we will bring together these elements as they relate to the character and message of the work.

The coordinates of language

The translation that appears in this volume attempts to maintain the linguistic and contextual authenticity of the original text. This unveiling of the stories to a new audience purports to preserve the author's unique perspective on action, description, dialogue and character development that acquaint the reader with divergent subjects related to matters of manhood.

Appropriate word choices and phraseology determine the translation's faithfulness to the tone and direction of the stories as well as the portrayal of the protagonists and their actions. This challenge contemplates use of proper or improper grammar constructions, idiomatic expressions, a mixture of English and Spanish, and ambiguity or innuendo as appropriate.

Deliberate use of incorrect grammar and/or stereotypical phrases help depict the nature of characters' voices. The original text employs these techniques as a mechanism for creating quick studies of the individuals being portrayed, especially in "Puerto Rican Parade," with its many lively dialogues that include spectators, parade participants, a politician and others. While each type-cast figure may not be the most positive role model, the intent is to demonstrate the breadth of humanity in the arch of the story. By presenting characters from all walks of life, the community in general becomes more diverse and all-inclusive.

The mixture of English and Spanish also has its place in translation. In stories with young protagonists such as "A Matter of Men," the translation preserves some references to family members in the original Spanish. There, the use of *abuelo* and *abuela* (grandfather and grandmother) resonate better in the voice of the eight-year-old narrator whose grandparents obviously lived in Cuba. In addition, the prosaic English equivalents take away from the poetic feel to the story.

The translation also preserves the names of saints and hurricanes in the original language. Throughout most of the text, slang was translated into English, with the exception of the use of the terms such as "*mamacita,*" part of a pick-up line in "Night on the Town." Whole Spanish phrases were left intact in very few places, primarily in "Puerto Rican Parade." Terms referring to Puerto Rico (*Borinquen*) and Puerto Rican (*Boricua*) were preserved as was the Spanish phrase attributed to the Mexican charro on horseback, where an English translation would have made this distinctive voice lose its contrast with the speech patterns of the parade's Puerto Rican participants.[1]

Several scenes in the translation also use measured poetic license due to the lack of parallel phrases or idiomatic expressions. For example, the use of logical oxymora (i.e.: locura cuerda = lucid madness), the rhymes in the lyrics in "Puerto Rican Parade" and the poetic elements of "Swarm" and "A Story to be Sung," approximate the experience in the original text by delving into the shading and emotional context of the stories.

While linguistic choices for description and dialogue are crucial, other queues are also vital to bringing the narrative to life. References to music, gestures, looks, aromas, mannerisms and other details are paramount for creating a mood or giving insight into the characters or the ambience of a given scene. In "A Matter of Men" non-verbal communication takes on one of the lead roles of the story. The father's furtive smile represents the secret joys of manhood. This seldom-seen expression is replicated on the faces of the mother and sister as they conceal their knowledge regarding what is about to befall the protagonist. In "Night on the Town" the narrator describes the colors and form of clothing, the shades and application of make-up, the power of a demure look, the bolero that incites dance and sensuality, the smell of cologne and the mounting tension in

---

[1] "Pues viva Puerto Rico no más, ándele pues." This phrase means: "Well, long live Puerto Rico—that's all, you know that's right."

the crescendo of emotions in an anticipated intimate encounter. In these two stories, a "look" or "smile" provide important, unspoken meaning. Throughout the book, these two words are imbued with a variety of semblances through the underlying frame of reference. The translation creates the background for these visages, infusing synonyms for these facial expressions to capture the tenor of the original text.

Thus, proper lexicon, voice and ambience provide authentic narratives and dialogues that set the stage for scenes, vignettes, tales and accounts that convey experiences that are common across cultures. Language creates the vehicle for shared enjoyment and enlightenment.

A matter of men—of all mankind

Benito Pastoriza Iyodo has openly admitted that his sense of story-telling is influenced by intensive observation of people as they interact within the framework of society.[2] The resulting narratives incorporate many elements and techniques used in contemporary cinema. Within modern literary and film production, works from different parts of the world and different social milieus are widely embraced. The use of characters with diverse social and ethnic backgrounds, national origins, disabilities, sexual orientations and economic classes need not restrict the broader applicability of the message of a book, story or movie. While some writing is meant to reflect local custom in a documentary style, a well-crafted work—no

[2] Perlman, Martin. "Benito Pastoriza: A Whore to the Word." *Santa Barbara News & Review* 12 Mar. 1981: 18-19.

Reed, Verlia Josette. "Indiscreet Charm: People watcher wins prize." *The Daily Cougar* 26 Jan. 1990: 7.

matter its language, spatial limitations or cast of characters—can yield a story and message that moves beyond the provincial or national. Oscar-winning movies have included the explosion of international turmoil caused by the gift of a rifle to a hunting guide [*Babel* (2006)], the intertwined lives of strangers [*Amores Perros* (2000) and *CRASH* (2004)], grappling with the issues of love and sexuality [*Transamerica* (2005) and *Brokeback Mountain* (2005)] and many other topics that may have been "local stories" but became ubiquitous in their message because of their treatment. Plots spanning short periods of time and characters portrayed as relatively ordinary people can provide insight into larger society and the decisions that we must all make. Many acclaimed works not only entertain; they make us think. We connect with them, even as we deny any commonality with the plot or the characters. We process their meaning, having our own beliefs confirmed or questioned. They may also inspire us to re-examine society, even if the narrative's conflict is "someone else's fault or problem."

When *A Matter of Men* was first published in December of 1996, several reviewers looked at the text through the eyes of the social consciousness of that era. While acknowledging that the collection was a polemic instrument that would shake things up, they took the book at its word and went no farther than to declare in the headline: "It's not easy to be a man."[3] But this collection of short stories goes far beyond the external queues used to frame the arch of the book. All of the images and characters are very transferable to other cultures. The book creates a world populated with protagonists that can be found in many societies.

These nine stories pose many questions: What is expected of a man? What is it to be a man—a worthy man—a man worth

---

3 "No es fácil ser hombre." *La Información* 20-26 Mar. 1997: 7.

educating—a man worth living—a man worth loving? Is it different for a Hispanic, Asian, black or white man? What if you are rich or poor? What if you are a professional or down on your luck? A super-macho or refined? A senator, educator, writer or ex-con? Eloquent or barely literate? What are the elements of manhood? How broad or narrow is the criteria? Who establishes the norm? With what right? And what is right?

The scholar, Dr. Carlos Manuel Rivera, writing about *A Matter of Men*, proclaimed that this collection of stories gives us a cultural vision from a more open point of view, in which a multitude of characters and voices stand out, leaving us incapable of delimiting them in terms of ethnic, linguistic, class or generic categories.[4]

But for another scholar, *A Matter of Men* is more than an exploration of male sexuality. Dr. Heidi Ann García presents a view of this collection of short stories that goes beyond bridging ethnicity and nationality. In a review, Dr. García wrote that these stories were presented "in a poetic manner, in diaphanous language with daring and innovative images, laying out the evolution of "man," from childhood through adulthood—not defined by age but through one's encounter with the Self." She considered the word "man," when referring to these stories, to represent all mankind, regardless of gender or sexual preference.[5]

4 Rivera, Carlos Manuel. "Cuestión de hombres: un estudio preliminar para su segunda edición." Pastoriza Iyodo, Benito. *Cuestión de hombres*. Philadelphia: Xlibris Corp., 2006. 23.

5 García, Heidi Ann. Reviews. "Pastoriza Iyodo, Benito. *Cuestión de hombres*. Bronx: Latino Press, 1996. 79 pp. ISBN 1-884-91208-7." *Chasqui; revista de literatura latinoamericana*. 35.2 (2006): 157-161, P 157.

This interpretation imbues *A Matter of Men* with a new aura of responsibility, a responsibility to pose questions addressing the definition, categorization and responsibility of all mankind, a responsibility addressed through the voice, dialogue, form and cinematic treatment of these narratives.

Voice, dialogue, form and cinematography

Introduction

Like a chameleon, Pastoriza Iyodo searches for the correct blend of tones and lighting, characters and emotion so that the story's point of view is genuine, yet camouflaged enough so that it is not overbearing. Most often he utilizes one of the principle characters in the story as the main voice of the narrative, sprinkling the journey with dialogue and/or the occasional omniscient narrator. Some stories are almost exclusively narrative: "Trash," "The Bag of Pleasures" and "Swarm," among others. Some are almost pure poetry in form, such as "Swarm" and "A Story to be Sung." All nine stories would lend themselves to cinematic treatment that might vary in length from a short scene (as in "Swarm") to a one-man theater piece or full-length film (such as "Night on the Town").

Voice and Presentation

"A Matter of Men" is told from the point of view of an eight-year-old boy. He narrates the story and recounts dialogues from family history or from his own personal experience. As the plot unfolds, it becomes evident that there are three main characters: the boy, his father and his father's smile, with the latter being the most mysterious and illusive of the three. Using the boy's voice as the focal point of this chronicle keeps the reader in as much suspense as the little boy who, like us, finds out about the mysteries of manhood as they are unveiled during the story.

"Trash" is told by a slightly older boy, revealing the more discerning voice of an adolescent. This story includes a variety of settings and activities from daily life that trigger much longer mini-vignettes in the mind of the reader, based on common observation or shared personal experiences. Here, more emphasis is put on narrative and description of place than on dialogue. Stereotyping plays a large role in this saga, with the title, "Trash," in its literal and figurative forms playing the lead. The references to refuse (post-consumption, comical, stereotypical and despicable) appear throughout the narrative, entertaining and appalling at the same time.

> Many times we could guess what was going on with our neighbors just by the trash they discarded. Egg shells, a Carnation can, sugar—they were preparing flan. Photographs, cigarettes, bottles—the lovers' quarrel had begun.

"The Bag of Pleasures" employs the voice of a youth of undetermined age, surviving without the aid of adults. While not the leader of the group, he remains the focal source of narrative and action in a very conflicted co-existence. This story presents a microcosm of society that reflects the struggle between isolated groups that seek to subsist and coexist even if it means acquiring the refuse discarded or hoarded by those possessing more.

"Good Morning Commensal" is told by an unidentified narrator who calls the play-by-play of the daily eating routine of a transient man. Almost all observers at the bus stop detest the ritual, but none does anything to remedy the situation. A commensal, by definition, shares a table with others, and from a purely biological standpoint, maintains a symbiotic relationship with other beings for his existence. The lead character of this chronicle is speechless, yet the story's action demonstrates his station in life. The reaction of "normal folks" to his joyous ritual of savoring discarded morsels provides a comic-tragic effect. The commensal, content with his banquet, seems pleased with the horror that his presence and actions strike in the "guiltless" onlookers.

"Puerto Rican Parade" includes the eloquent narration of a media broadcaster in stark contrast to dialogues that occur among participants on floats, spectators in the streets, politicians, educators and others. The dialogue in this story stresses the contradiction between reality and the broadcaster's idyllic description of the parade, Puerto Rico and its people. These mini-vignettes—rather than stereotyping—present parodies of the characters, demonstrating the vast array of personality types that exist in any society or nationality. Depending on the person being portrayed, there may be linguistic shifts to approximate an attitude, social status or educational level. But Pastoriza presents these characters without passing judgment on them. He offers complex questions and images to his readers in a very simple and entertaining fashion, forcing the reader to come to his or her own conclusion as to the righteousness, intelligence, authenticity or irony of the situation. This technique also shows how the privileged can see themselves and others through a different lens when contrasted with observations made by others with fewer resources.

"Romantic Disgrace" is about the expectations of a woman: what she expects of a man, what she expects to consume and how both should affect her. The majority of the narration vacillates between the leading lady's thoughts and an omniscient narrator. The sparse dialogue punctuates the comedic aspects of this adventure.

> —Who has change?
> —Lady it takes bills.
> —No way! I worked hard to get this greenback, mopping the stinking floors of those bankrupt rich folks. Who has change? No one here eats or drinks? Where's the change they gave you at the store?
> —Here lady, take this.
> —No way! I don't want a handout. I work from sunrise to sunset. But since you insist . . .

Despite the protagonist's prime-time informed astuteness and devotion to better living through the use of the latest innovation, she finds it necessary to depend on her bargain-hunting skills to attempt to fill the void of her own expectations.

"Night on the Town" is told by one of the two leading protagonists. This is perhaps the most cinematic of all the stories. It is rich with dialogue and description that includes action, music, glances and adventure. It uses the cinematographic device of beginning at the end, then narrating the events and dialogues that led to the opening sequence. In the recounted story, the action occurs in a series of well-defined scenes with numerous characters. The description, narrated thoughts and dialogues tell a linear story that leads to a conflict of social norms. A flurry of events shared by two friends on an adventure ends in tragedy, with the narrator facing the results of a night on the town.

The last two stories reflect two types of love, told by two different voices. In "Swarm" the omniscient voice describes the act of making love without a single break in the story. There is no punctuation throughout this narrative and it is meant to evoke the frenzy of the act being described without using any vernacular phrases or vulgarity. It is truly an erotically poetic whirlwind.

By contract, "A Story to be Sung" is told by a character who discovers love through a series of happenings that firmly implants the *idea* of love, transforms this anticipation into its physical manifestation and explores the definition and attributes of that love. The first of four parts of the story was particularly difficult to translate, as it dealt with the appearance of an anticipated love that makes visits even before he exists. This concept holds more poetic sway in Spanish, so the translation preserves the Spanish title "el prefigurado"—"the anticipated one." The Prefigurado becomes flesh in "beginning" and "angela's café." In the final segment of this story, the relationship matures as each discovers the essence of the other, little by little, as if exploring nature itself.

> Here the leaves accumulate along our path. Exploring them we discover a time not our own, somewhat diluted by the passing minutes, imprecise hours, stagnant hours. These long walks led me to know your life, a labyrinth of lights that have enclosed the air, the wind that defines existence.

Conclusion

Benito Pastoriza Iyodo's work is crafted in images that capture the light and shadows of contemporary life. *A Matter of Men* questions why certain norms and hypocrisy exist. Some of the images and narratives employed shock us while others delight. Pastoriza Iyodo is a truth seeker—idealistic in his expectations and realistic in his world view. He commits his readers to the conspiracy of seeking truth, which may provide moments of joy and elation as well as sadness and tragedy.

In either case, two themes come through in *A Matter of Men*: (1) mankind defines the mechanisms of control; and (2) we acquiesce to the status quo or challenge it within the framework of our own valor. As Dr. García states, "In the end, only the 'man' who is capable of loving another and dares to manifest it; he who confronts his fears and, in spite of them, lives and makes himself ONE with his surroundings; he who lives and feels his equality with the whole universe, is the one who becomes a MAN."[6]

Pastoriza Iyodo takes the axiom "love is for the valiant" and imprints it on his literature as his unique brand, implying that "only the strong can face the truth." Another maxim that may be applied to several of the works in this collection comes from Amado Nervo. This Mexican philosopher and poet proclaims: " . . . I was the architect of my own destiny; . . . Life, you owe me nothing!"[7] The theme of societal norms, stereotypes and expectations are juxtaposed with the reality in which the characters of the stories find themselves. At times the narratives

---

6 García, Heidi Ann. Reviews. "Pastoriza Iyodo, Benito. *Cuestión de hombres*. Bronx: Latino Press, 1996. 79 pp. ISBN 1-884-91208-7." *Chasqui; revista de literatura latinoamericana*. 35.2 (2006): 157-161, P 158.

7 Nervo, Amado. "EN PAZ." *Antología poética e ideario de Amado Nervo*. México: Editores Mexicanos Unicos, S.A, 1992: 49.

reflect the aspirations, decisions made and valor displayed by the protagonists within the framework of the larger society. Their decisions, made in the face of diverse challenges, affect their own lives and the lives of others. These narratives pose many questions: What are the weaknesses of our society? What choices do we have? Why is there hardship? Who is responsible? Why so much pigeon-holing? What causes man's inhumanity to man? What causes hypocrisy: pressure to live within the norms or cowardice?

For millennia humans have invented and re-invented the definition of mankind and the relationship of man to man and male to female as well as man's role in the universe—regarding nature and divinity. Many cultures throughout the globe have adopted a patriarchal view of the power struggles inherent in these relationships. This world-view is reflected in all aspects of our lives: in our governments, politics, economics and foreign affairs as well as our continual denial of our share of responsibility for causing society's ills. All of this to show strength, to preserve man's own power and to exercise control.

In this collection, "man" searches for his soul in his culture and rituals, in the violence of the cities and its institutions, in the stereotypes imposed upon him, in the misguided interpretations of mass media and the judgment of others. We can choose to read these nine stories as narratives that make us laugh, lament, whence or celebrate. At the same time we can ponder the questions and issues lurking among the scenic mangroves along the shadowy path of discovery.

A MATTER OF MEN

My father only smiled when he was alone. It was difficult to coax a grin from that rough-hewn, country face. Mama got furious when she caught him laughing in front of the mirror as if, at that moment, his reflection had just told him the joke of the year. She, who could never get the corners of his mouth to turn up, did not understand this ritual of joy and solitude that delighted papa so. He carried his happiness within, like someone who indulges in something secretly without the rest of the world finding out.

In those days, when I had just turned eight, he started looking at me with a strange smile, as if trying to include me in the marvels of his world. At first I thought my father was starting to see himself in me, the continuation of his lineage, the childlike reflection of his being—the duplication of his life that in some form would end up in me, in this boy who got away with everything, without a scolding, without a spanking. Because for him life was made up of brief encounters and his son had arrived to enjoy intensely this fleeting moment of existence.

Papa had died when he was seven in Pinar del Río, a coastal town north of Havana. Nine days later he was resuscitated after an arduous fight between life and death. The santeros, with their shells and stones, brought him back from the underworld of the sea where his soul had gone to rest. Abuela, who bore eleven girls trying for a boy, left no stone unturned to gain the return of her beloved macho.

When papa gasped the breath of life this second time, Abuela promised Santa Barbara that she would never be separated from her son again. Until he was eighteen he slept with Abuela and Abuelo. At night, when he stretched out his legs, he could feel the impassioned rubbing of their bodies, her soft moans pleading for a speedy climax due to the boy's presence. The boy was already learning the tricks of lovemaking.

Papa's strange smile began to follow me everywhere. He even hung around the bathroom, where I performed my cleaning ritual, as if looking for some secret, something I guarded that he would discretely discover. My visits to the bathroom became more sporadic and unexpected so papa would not find out about my silent groans or the tears I swallowed because of the unbearable pain that came from between my legs. He imagined something was wrong; I could sense it in my father's smile, his faithful accomplice.

Mama, on the other hand, was always more direct in her approach. Subtleties were not part of her emotional make-up. She always reminded us that she had been born the night of San Ciprian, and that terrible hurricane, that had devastated the island, would remain inside her for the rest of her days. She calculated, measured, and estimated the value of everything. Odors and tastes never eluded her. Everything was scrutinized, examined, turned over and over again. She was a merchant's daughter and did not lose any time beating around the bush. "I call a spade a spade," she said when she wanted to get right to the point. "And you, why do you spend so much time in the bathroom and why have you started washing your own underwear?"

The answer was absolute silence.

Days later they both got up with the same expression—that inviolable smile, the one that could not be deciphered. My father was a man of few words and each mandate carried great meaning. He approached me and whispered in my ear, "Son, at some time you will have to become a man and it's not always when you want to." The words pronounced my sentence. They had discovered my secret; the intimate agony of my suffering was exposed without my knowing where it would lead.

The day I was to die I was playing checkers with my sister. She was obviously trying to let me win and her acting was not very convincing. We always fought over every move, accusing each other of cheating—invention of our crazy imaginations—all to further our schemes for victory. That day I noticed that out of contagion or pity, she wore the same smirk as my parents. She avoided arguments and behaved herself in an exaggeratedly kind manner. The silence learned from my father would not let me ask her the question. She always knew what was going on; she always had an answer for everything. But curiosity won out and I got up my nerve.

—Will it hurt?

—Will what hurt?

—Will death hurt?

—Papa never told me if it hurt or not.

—Will I be the same?

—They say that after you die you're reborn as a man, I don't know.

—And what will I die of?

—You're going to die of the same thing as everyone else, you'll die of death.

I never understood why they dressed me in my Sunday best to meet my death. Mama delighted in seeing me dressed in white. She was overwhelmed with joy and she dressed me such zeal, as if I were going to meet the Pope. The shorts, which I hated, went with the white linen shirt that matched my shoes of the same color. The best part of the ritual was getting to use papa's cologne; to smell like him was a privilege given on very few occasions. "This is my macho," she said after dressing me with great care like one of my sister's dolls.

Papa took my hand with a firm grip and with a voice that seemed to come from a great distance he said, "Let's go and become men." The country roughness returned to his face and the smile, which intrigued me so much, disappeared. For the duration of the trip he did not say a single word and it seemed as if he were trying to swallow lumps of iron that had lodged in his throat.

Upon arriving, we sat patiently in the waiting room, where people with sad faces came and went. I noticed that some of the people, dressed all in white like me, looked at me with curiosity, or perhaps complicity. One of them approached us and very solemnly said, "The doctor is ready for him." Papa squeezed my hand harder than ever, almost to the point of hurting me.

Everything happened so fast, yet so slowly. The ladies in white began to undress me while the doctor put on a cloth that covered his face. Another one neared with a tray covered with scissors and strange knives. I started to cry. Now naked, they placed me on a cold metal table where they opened my legs wide apart. They secured my legs with belts to make sure that I couldn't move. I heard when the man with the mask told my papa, "This is a routine procedure and is done without anesthesia." My shrieks began to bounce off the walls. "I hate you papa. I hate you."

The initial incision hurt the most. My tears and my screams weren't enough to express the pain and humiliation I felt. I spit at the doctor while he cut and cut my insides without stopping. Every cut intensified the pain. Papa sweated and bit his lips while I yelled at him at the top of my lungs, "Papa, get me out of here, I'll be good; I'll be good."

The voyage to hell would not end. Time stood still in that room. When I heard the doctor say—needle—the world broke into millions of pieces. My body, wet with sweat, could find no more tears or screams to dowse the pain. Worn out, I could only whimper non-stop while that needle perforated my bloody skin.

The nightmare of meeting death ended with a bath. The ladies in white invaded my insides with alcohol that burned the most hidden parts of my weakened body. They dressed me in my white Sunday suit and I was instructed to walk with my legs very open so I would not feel the post-operative pain. "You can take this one away. Now he can make a family and enjoy life. Bring him back in a month to cut the stitches."

Enjoy life. My father carried me in his arms as if caring for a wounded dove. I began to bleed lightly. A fine red line began to form on my white shorts. Enjoy life. The red dripping began to dampen my father's arm. I observed how his forehead sweated and his eyes seemed to float stagnant in a great pool of water. Enjoy life. His arms trembled strangely. He could barely walk without stumbling. I, submerged in pain, felt that something faded away; something inside had died. I tried to find that smile, my father's accomplice that would include me in the wonder of his world, in the promised pleasure of becoming a man, feeling the enormous door that would open to the life that lay ahead.

TRASH

The day it first rained trash we had just arrived from Puerto Rico. Mama, as usual, was excited about starting her new enterprises, which represented our future return to the island at the expense of years of her arduous labor. She set a clear goal, "Honey, I'm going to work, and work hard; and in less than three years we'll be on our way back." She seemed obliged to explain herself constantly, repeating the same phrase to my sister with only a slight variation, "Sweetheart, don't worry, don't cry. This won't last long." My sister had been blubbering ever since we got off the plane; letting intermittent outbursts escape, "I hate him, I hate him; I hate him with all my might!"

My father did not dare look at us. He was withdrawn, deep within his own sense of guilt; and for the rest of his years he would never again be able to look us straight in the eyes. You see, he always had a weakness for women. Back in Cuba they had given him a nickname, the aimless pony, because he went from one mare to another. During his bachelor days he bragged about his conquests with the pride of a handsome macho. It pained him to settle down during those first few years of matrimony, and then . . . he started prancing again. This latest gallop was with Lydia, a lover who knew full well the art of seduction. She had succeeded in taming the pony, to the point of wrenching the family's last penny from his willing hand.

My mother's enthusiasm for her new endeavors blinded her to the surroundings that we were to call home. It was a decrepit building on a street teeming with drug addicts and traffickers armed to the teeth. The doors on the mail boxes had been forced open leaving exposed any welfare check that might be delivered. This explained why every Monday morning all the welfare mothers met on the stoop of the building to wait for their beloved don Welfare, as they often referred to the source of their financial support. The hallway was a long tunnel that reeked of urine. Halfway down its length it was lit by a tiny light bulb, which only illuminated a small circumference around it. Upon entering this time tunnel each potential victim became an actor. You had to sprint from the entrance to the halo of light, where, like being on stage, nothing was discernible in any direction, blinded by the light and exposed by the darkness. A short dash further led to our apartment door made of a durable, thief-proof metal.

Our apartment was magical. Every inch was filled with the light that came from the large windows of its three rooms. The central room served as kitchen, dining room and bathroom. We found it amusing to discover that one only need remove the lid that camouflaged the bathtub to transform the dining room table into the center of our daily hygiene. We ate and bathed in the same room, and from there we could jump to our bedroom to watch Batman or to the living room (my parents' bedroom) to watch it rain garbage. Through the enormous windows we could make out the small courtyard that lay less than six feet below the level of our balcony. The courtyard was filling with trash, which would reach our balcony in a matter of another three feet. It was like watching a pool filling up, not with water, but with garbage.

The primary purpose of the balconies was as a means of escape in case of a fire, but our neighbors liked to use them to sunbathe, to fly kites, to drink beer and sometimes . . . to make love—preferably at night, when they thought everybody was asleep. But everyone in the neighborhood knew about these live shows, especially when the protagonists started shouting and moaning as if they were in the privacy of their own beds. When this happened someone would invariably throw pails of cold water on the steamy couple to cool them off.

Our neighbors led diverse and agitated lives. From their balconies it rained condoms, bloody syringes, cans, Pepsi cola, kotex, reused pampers, boxes of cheerios, cotton balls stained with blood, beef stew, pasteles, chicken and rice, Goya products, Don Q, records by Daniel Santos, La Lupe, and Olga Guillot; love letters, TV dinners, lettuce, tomato, avocados, poems, pencils, photos of strange persons, magazines with pictures of naked people in strange positions, cigarettes, ashtrays, Colgate, combs, hair spray, soap, ham, cardboard, sausages, dogs, cats, birds, *Buen Hogar*, *Vanidades*, toys, dolls, dildos, saliva, salsa, garlic, onion, parsley, cheese, roaches and lots of rats, lots of live rats swimming in this sea of refuse. Many times we could guess what was going on with our neighbors just by the trash they discarded. Egg shells, a Carnation can, sugar—they were preparing flan. Photographs, cigarettes, bottles—the lovers' quarrel had begun.

We did not like it one bit when our folks got the horrible idea that it was time for us to start going to school. This meant having to learn English, a language that was totally foreign to us. The first day was torture. We listened to the English teacher talk about this guy, Othello, who was black like us Puerto Ricans and the other blacks in the class. The poor fellow didn't know what he wanted out of life—and the class really cut up: throwing paper wads, chalk and erasers at the lily white teacher.

The Spanish teacher was a Chinese man who had a terrible time pronouncing all the R's in our last names. That day he was set on teaching us the ABC's and we couldn't convince him that we had learned that lesson many years before. After going to the academic classes, we were assigned to various workshops according to our respective nationalities: the Asians to the science lab, the blacks to the mechanic shop and the Latinos to carpentry. I spent three hours learning how to make a ridiculous tie rack. When I gave it to my father, he looked at me with a curious smile, unable to explain how they had gotten such a useless article out of a bookworm like me.

Leaving school that first day, my sister noticed that a man was following us. We quickened our pace and made a detour from our planned route. We lost him; he was nowhere in sight. When we got back to our building we saw one of the welfare mothers patiently waiting for the mailman. Her presence made us feel a bit less afraid. We were ready to enter the hallway we knew as the time tunnel; "enter today but you won't come out tomorrow," when the lady rushed over to stop us. "Don't go in there. Some guy has been in there for a while. I don't know if he's shooting up or waiting for you guys." Sure enough, after she described him, it sounded like the same man who had been following us. My sister, who was in the throws of puberty, started to panic. She thought that he was after her. We couldn't dissuade her and she almost went into one of her infamous tantrums.

It was getting dark when our protector decided to go into the hall alone. She wanted to make sure that the coast was clear. She returned with an unconvincing smile, "It looks like that guy took off using the roof 'cause I didn't see hide nor hair of him anywhere." She accompanied us and we arrived at our door a bit calmer; we unlocked the four deadbolts on the door and entered what we thought would be the safety of our magic apartment. As she bid us good-bye, the smile disappeared from her face, which we chalked up to fatigue from having to wait such a long time with us on the stoop.

As we entered we heard some noise, but then we remembered that in this building it rained trash and it was probably some can falling into the courtyard. We were still so nervous that it took a while for us to find the light switch. When we finally found it, the light revealed a white floor dotted with large rats running like crazy in all directions. Our first instinct was to climb on top of the dining table/bathtub cover to observe the spectacle with horror. My sister signaled me to look through the windows and indeed, the trash had reached the level of our balcony.

Now we were becoming part of all that waste. All around us other people's filth piled up: bottles, excrement, plastic, mud, spoiled meat, broken glass, and a sea of objects that had lost their form and purpose. Among the rubbish dangling from the balcony we could make out a pair of long legs that contracted strongly as the intruder strained to open the enormous window that barely separated us from that garbage bin. Then we recognized his face as belonging to the man who had followed us earlier. My sister looked at me desperately as if her life were going to end right then and there. In her expression I saw the terror of a defenseless animal besieged by a relentless stalker. That nightmare silenced the air, and only my sister's sobbing could be heard, growing in intensity, her stifled weeping voice screamed out her morbid litany, "I hate him, I hate him, I hate him."

THE BAG OF PLEASURES

When I wake up at night, from my dark corner I can see the enormous rats swimming in a puddle of mud. At first they frightened me because they reminded me of the time we felt thousands of their little feet crawling all over our bodies. It all started with the little fat girl's birthday party and Pachín's idea of spying on promising festivities.

We had spent all day looking for food in the trash containers when, at last, we came upon a huge family having a picnic with lots and lots of food. The plates were overflowing with tacos, enchiladas, salads, meat, beans and an excessive quantity of tortillas. We knew right away that there would be plenty of food left over and plastic bags would be filled with delicious home-made delights. It was just a matter of waiting. As they sang happy birthday to the fat girl with melon-colored cheeks we spied the rose-colored cake topped with strawberries and cream, crowned with a plastic doll that looked like the birthday girl. That day we really had it made.

A little later the piñata exploded after a strong, husky boy gave the blue, paper burro a mighty whack; and the girl, who was nearby also felt the wallop. The girl cried profusely as the rest of the children scampered about looking for candy. We kept mental notes on the locations of pieces that rolled far from the feverish search so we could retrieve them later from their resting places. Our intestines were grumbling as the family finally began to say good-bye to all their friends and relatives.

The good-bye lasted almost as long as the party—or at least it seemed that way to the clocks in our stomachs. We were overjoyed when we saw that Mrs. Clean (every party has one) did not empty the plates, putting the food in a separate bag. She threw the paper plates into a bag, with the food still intact. The food had been served; it would be a matter of taking the plates out of the bag and chowing down. As soon as the family left, we carefully took out three or four plates and started to savor those leftovers, which tasted succulent after days without eating.

Quite a bit of food was left and it was Pachín's idea to take it back to the tunnel that night. We had to watch out to make sure the others were gone so they wouldn't find out about the treasure we had discovered; food enough for at least three days. By that time I also knew about the rats, but from afar. I had learned to avoid them, go around them, without venturing too deeply into this subterranean world that also belonged to them. Pachín thought we should guard the food by keeping it at the head of the sleeping mat; so if anyone else got too close, we could trap them. So when we lay down the bag was almost on top of our heads.

It was already night and with our stomachs full, a damned sleep overcame us. It's not advisable to sleep in this world. When we fell asleep in the other drain pipe, something always happened that brought us closer to death. In the sewer of the Coyotes, Pachín decided to sleep one night and they gave us a terrible beating and took over the place. We bled for a couple of days and my face wouldn't heal. The gash they gave me covered half my cheek and it looked like one of those half moons that comes out on nights when things are only partially lit.

I hadn't yet fallen into a sound sleep when I felt a tickle on the bottom of my foot. I didn't pay any attention, thinking that it was Pachín playing one of his tricks on me again and I closed my eyes to let that dangerous sleep take me over. Later I felt a heavy object on my behind. From there it began emitting strange sounds as if it were communicating with its troops. The sounds paralyzed me. I tried to move, but my state of panic wouldn't let me breathe. I thought about the last beating we'd received, about my scarred face, about how many there would be. Pachín slept like a log. There was no way to know how many rats were on my body. Out of the corner of my eye I could see a rat scratching at Pachín's nostril. Its pointed teeth played with what it took from his nasal passages. I couldn't utter a sound, nor scream, nor howl. My own fear frightened me.

Then I felt some fifteen rats climbing up and down my side and back. The bag had already been broken open and they carried off the treasure of the party we had spied on. I felt their claws scrape against my face, piercing the skin of my scalp. My immobile body had turned into a highway to their sustenance. Some were so large and fat that they could barely move about and I could feel the slowness with which they carried their weight toward the bag. And Pachín was in a world of dreams, snoring as if nothing were happening. His mouth, open from snoring, was a necessary stop for the rats that passed by. I tried to scream, but fear paralyzed every attempt to save myself.

I had already seen a girl die of rabies in the tunnel. The rat had bitten her the first day she entered the sewer. Pregnant by one of the kids in the barrio, she had fled her family home. She couldn't deal with the shame of being pointed out so she joined us in here. At first she seemed courageous, but hours later the poor thing shivered with fear and cold, as if they had transported her to the worst of nightmares. Her body gave in rapidly to the illness and a few days later death took her away with her stomach of a mother-to-be that was already showing.

That agonizing face was burned in my memory as the paws of the rats ran rapidly over my back. Pachín, wake up, Pachín, I repeated to myself in the silence of my mind. It seemed as if my friend were possessed by all the slumber in the world, when I noticed him open an eye and he winked as a warning to stay alert. We had our own secret signals and this one meant to run like crazy, come what may. On the second wink we jumped up like furious monsters in an unbridled gallop that seemed to scare dozens of rats that fell from our bodies.

Now every night I watch them from my dark corner. I see them wriggle and climb one on top of the other. I hear them whisper age-old curses. It has even amused me. I have learned to sleep while remaining awake, to swim in the silence of the sewer, to smell food in the emptiness of the void. To perceive with my little eyes the arrival of the other hoard in the darkness.

GOOD MORNING COMMENSAL

Every day he would come there to eat his breakfast. The bus stop, a futuristic glass box, served as his public dining room amidst the eleven people squeezed together waiting for the bus. He discretely accommodated himself among them to make sure that all eyes would be directed toward his persona. If a strategic space was lacking, he would sit on the ground, and looking straight ahead, he would start his dining ritual. He glared at each one of us individually, attentively fixed on any grimace that confessed some level of disapproval. With special care he peeled a ripe plantain, set it to one side, and then with feline deliberateness, he opened his can of generic cat food.

There was a different flavor for each day, but every Monday he delighted in a can of tuna, Wednesday's flavor was chicken, and on Fridays—mixed variety. The recalcitrant odor permeated the cubicle and the whole area acquired a dizzying stench that only let up when a cold wind came to the rescue or one of the ladies took out a bottle of perfume, pretending that it was time to apply a touch-up of her favorite fragrance. On a few occasions one of the patrons would smoke before his arrival to dissipate the fumes a bit. This irritated his Karma to no end, since it clashed with his customary morning ritual.

First he caught a whiff of the fumes of the ground meat like an animal trying to identify what he was about to eat. It was like a carnivorous sampling, savoring the aroma before digging into the flavorful meat. Later, the vapors having been well-sniffed, he drank the juice with such suction that the excessive racket reached the next stop where the future passengers pricked up their ears like radar to ascertain what the uproar was all about. Now his pinkie finger would take charge of the rest. He had sharpened what there was of a fingernail, sucking on it to remove the remaining residue from the nail so that his little finger could become a clean, human spoon. He scraped out small portions that went directly to his tongue where he continued categorizing and relishing each morsel. He licked his lips with delight and from time to time he smiled at his spectators, showing his gap-toothed mouth covered with granules that refused to dissolve. The next instant he gulped down a piece of the over-ripe plantain to wash down the rest of the cat food.

That culinary delight closed with a detailed search of the nearby garbage can, his paradise of free provisions; let's see what he would find: a half finished can of soda—down the hatch; a bag with two potato chips—let's see if they're still crunchy; partially used napkins for later; cigarette butts with a couple of puffs still left; cans, cans, and more cans; a cockroach, some bees but they don't sting; ants . . . ants . . . ants; plastic wrap, bottles, newspapers—the good housekeeping section always makes good reading; cans and more cans and at the very bottom he spies something. What is this? The little miracle of the day, a can of tuna that's hardly been touched—and brand name at that. He covers it carefully in discarded plastic wrap and with a smile bigger than all outdoors, he bids us adieu with a good day and see you tomorrow.

PUERTO RICAN PARADE

Esteemed radio listeners, television audience and other dignified observers of this magnificent Puerto Rican Parade; I, Pepe de la Gran Peña, your congenial and distinguished announcer, declare that the rain has ceased and we can see a ray of sunshine. At last, my dear and attentive public, there will be a Puerto Rican Parade in this most beautiful city of skyscrapers. Thank you oh great omnipotent Father, King of the Heavens, for having closed the celestial floodgates. It seems that the firmament is clearing up and we're starting off this magnanimous parade with nothing less than the national anthem of North America, performed by the marching band from Roberto Clemente High School, Athens of Puerto Rican bilingual learning in our beloved city. What execution and tempo they display playing the epic song of the nation that has protected us in good times and in bad; now Clemente High plays it with immense pride and marches with admirable solemnity.

So much Puerto Rican beauty parades down these silver city streets, here before us, the press, the judges and others of the upper crust. The queen, Miss Clemente High, passes dressed in the latest fashion of the distinguished designer Osvaldo de las Pesas. How majestic, supremely elegant, totally drenched by the rain, but she doesn't complain, as if nothing had happened, such grace ladies and gentlemen, I tell you that we are all nobility, all nobility.

—Look bro, I made it with that looker in the heat of the action at the dance last night, hey bro I really got off on that.

—They say she was higher than a kite after drinking that Spanish fly and that Spanish come-on.

—Nobody could understand a word she said with all that Mary Jane, something about her pa having big bucks and political connections, that's how she got to be in the parade. But I ain't buyin' that story.

—Look how she's all high and mighty, she won't even look at you, as if she didn't even know you.

—Aye mamita, from looking at you, who would know you? . . . Yesterday yours was a different kingdom.

Next and in no less monarchical hierarchy comes Miss Rumbera del Sabor dancing our unmistakable salsa, which has already become a favorite rhythm on the international scene. Where don't people listen to salsa? Paris, Munich, Stockholm, Barcelona, Tokyo; yes sir, even in Japanese they play that rhythm. Observe the refinement, the contour with which she moves her hips to and fro, and all this sponsored by Jewel Food Stores the supermarket of the Latinos where you can find the best meats to the appetizing delight of your husband's excellent taste.

What a beautiful flag, what a beautiful flag
what a beautiful flag, the Puerto Rican flag
even more beautiful, even more beautiful
even more beautiful if here it were not spit on.

—I've been telling you that you can't take these people out in public, look at that guy wiping his nose with the flag. How awful! How terrible.

> What a beautiful flag, what a beautiful flag

—I tell you that this is the height of indecency, look at how that gal dries her most intimate and private parts with what's left of the flag. How awful! How terrible!

> What a beautiful flag, what a beautiful flag
> what a beautiful flag, the flag of Puerto Rico.

And all the people dress in their three-color, lone star, immaculate flag—long live Puerto Rico ladies and gentlemen; and this most beautiful cloth that carries our supreme insignia as the most valiant and hard-fighting people of all times. Long live our Miss Universes: one, two and three that with perseverance carried their beauty and that of their people in this fabric that represents the Boriqua nation.

—So many flags, bro, cool, what a wild party and you didn't even want to come.

—Don't mess with me; look how that guy wears it on the back of his socks, and that other one painted it on his underwear.

—I guess that one's cold 'cause he's all wrapped up in one.

—Look, that guy's got balls; he's even painted it on his face and has the star smack in the middle of his schnozzle.

—Hey, cute gringa, kiss me. I'm Puerto Rican—Have some fun, mamita. Don't leave me like this with my lips puckered. I'm all yours, todito tuyo, Porto Rican for a day.

What regal splendor dear, respected TV audience! The city is brimming with joy to receive the authentic beauties from the island of enchantment. From the historic Castle of San Felipe del Morro the three princesses greet us with their unequaled and captivating smiles.

They represent three very noble coastal cities: in incandescent ruby red—the always passionate city of San Juan, in diaphanous gold chiffon—the exquisite pearl that is the city of Ponce and completing the arch of precious objects, the magnanimous and sultan city of the west, Mayagüez, in silver lame spangled with small diamonds.

—Oh damn, my feet are killing me from standing here so long, and all this to please my father; because if I don't, they won't give me the Ferrari.

—Smile dear, smile, this is why we paid an arm and a leg, to put you up there in your crystal palace, to show these uncultured masses that we're more from here than we are from over there.

—I detest this horrible cardboard castle. Who got the idea of building this incredibly ugly monstrosity? And then I have to smile as if I really liked being way up here.

—Smile, girlfriend, smile. We are truly the definition of beauty; look at how these country bumpkins stand there with their mouths wide open. Don't you love it? We're the best of Colgate, Palmolive and Fresh Star.

—We're all nobility; the announcer just said so again. Smile girlfriend, smile; pretend that this comes easy for us.

And above all, fine spectators—to be bilingual. Yes, my dear public, one must have complete command of these two great languages: English and Spanish. This will lead us to progress, to a good future and the peace of mind we so desire.

EL INGLÉS IS YOUR FUTURE—and how well it's announced on the Puerto Rican Educators' float with its immense Statue of Liberty carrying a book that reads STUDY ENGLISH TODAY BE HAPPY TOMORROW. I tell you there's nothing, nothing like enjoying yourself in two tongues.

—Did you fill out the application to the board you were so excited about?

—Go figure. They didn't cut me no slack and because I didn't know how to spick or spel good the language. They telled me I ain't got no idea about the student population of the area—after I burned the midnight oil for four years in college.

—I think the problem is you ain't got noone to push you for the position.

—No, I've done my networking. I even lunched with the head honcho.

—Don't you worry, I'll give him a ring and as they say, you'll be off and running.

And what Puerto Rican doesn't like a good beer, especially if it's a Bud Light, the beer of the Latinos in the United States. The proud sponsor of the scholarships for our future intellectuals and scientists, there's nothing like a Bud at your parties, baptisms, weddings, anniversaries, engagements, sweet sixteen's, confirmations, communications, meetings, graduations, birthdays, Christmas bashes, asaltos, social Fridays, excursions, Hispanic Day, Constitution Day, Independence Day, Associated Free State Day, Presidents' Day, Secretary's Day, Teacher's Day, and today, for the grand day of the Puerto Rican Parade—we can't do without the cold one—remember it's always time to enjoy, enjoy and enjoy even more.

—Listen; let me tell you the story of the drunk who had hallucinations after his fourth Bud Light . . .

—Go ahead; let's see if I already know it.

—A drunk goes walking by the Puerto Rican parade and comes upon this phlegm ball on the ground and says—"Oh my God what a beautiful gold medallion"—and when he goes to pick it up . . . he says full of surprise—"oh look, it even has a chain."

—Looks like you're as vulgar as ever; let's see if those police coming this way inspire a little decency in you, even if it's only for a while.

This splendid parade couldn't be without the Puerto Rican police or the Boricua firefighters. They are present in the raids, the riots, street confrontations, domestic disputes, shoot-outs and other minor crimes where they are likely to display their sophisticated training, but it's not that these things occur much in our community—to the contrary, you could count them on your fingers. Anyway we shouldn't even talk about anything negative during this parade. Because yes, ladies and gentlemen here present—there are noble Boricua police and firefighters here in the United States of America. What pride for our nation! Look at how our firemen come dancing the plena, look how they play the conga. Isn't it just grand?

—Hey big fella, I bet you can't put out my fire.

When the women
tease all the men
they show a lot of tit
and waive them
'round our balls

—Hey big fella, how vulgar. What I really want is for you to put out my fire and handcuff me like this . . . real smooth.

So desperate, so desperate
What'll become of this woman
when the big rod comes?

*Within our well-cultured community financial harmony reigns where there's no lack of cash and generous checks are always on the horizon. Thanks for sure to Colonial Mortgage Banker, presented before us as part of the group from the Puerto Rican Chamber of Commerce Club, distinguished and honored compatriots of the best businesses that take pride in saying—**HERE, YES HERE WE ACCEPT FOOD STAMPS.***

—Aye girlfriend, if it weren't for food stamps I'd really be screwed, with five mouths to feed and that husband of mine who is such a slacker that he wouldn't do a lick of work to save his own life.

—Listen girl, you don't know what I wouldn't give to go back to the island, but you know the saying, Puerto Rico thrills me but welfare fills me.

—But you really are dense, why go back to the island if everything's worse there? What, with the crime, the drugs, AIDS, the unemployment, the drought, the floods, the traffic jams, the corruption, the gangs, the pollution . . . No way. Don't you read El Vocero? . . . You're so uncultured.

—God bless you. But girl, there's nothing like the homeland: the beaches, the mountains, the people, the food . . .

—The beaches are polluted, dirty, and full of petroleum; the mountains have been eliminated to build highways and subdivisions; and that thing about the people: they're all closed in and no one sees hide nor hair of anyone on account of the crime, you imbecile. I tell you, you should read El Vocero. Wise up girlfriend.

My colleagues, my colleagues! Yes ladies and gentlemen, right here in front of us are parading the different television channels with the procession being led by nothing less than the reporters from Channel 44, the Hispanic Channel: the channel that brings joy. Because in the news everything is happiness in our beautiful Puerto Rico: the next international mayors' convention, the new Miss Universe, the recent increases in governmental salaries, Miss Puerto Rico International wins in Stockholm, statehood is almost a sure thing, more erotic programs on the TV. What joy for the nation—yes ladies and gentlemen! They really named us well—Puerto Rico! And what do my eyes see? Its the Boricua militia, the Puerto Rican military—uniforms, uniforms, uniforms—how valiant, how handsome, there's nothing like Boricua skin in a North American uniform and they take care of us even here in the United States. How well our young men march—uniforms, uniforms, uniforms.

A parade is not a parade my dear TV audience without the top representatives from the federal government.—And with great pride we present you on this spectacular and historic day to the first Puerto Rican senator in the White House, del Valle our first senator in White House, graduate of the Harvard University School of Law, born and raised in the barrio, truly an example of the American Dream, here for you all, because you asked for him and voted for him, our triumphant del Valle, del Valle, del Valle—our great American senator. Applause, applause, applause . . . yes, of course . . . Let's all stand up before this illustrious figure of Puerto Rican politics.

—How does my tie look?

—You look regal, impeccable as always, but smile a little more and wave at those people on the stage—they're businessmen.

—Did you make the appointment with the hairstylist and the tailor?

—Everything is set. You'll be like new tomorrow, a new look—a new image. Let's see if the voters start to forget about the affair you had with Alfonso. I regret having ever introduced him to you. We'll take some photos of you with María Luisa and the children and you'll be right as rain. The public has the memory of a mosquito.

—Did they finish writing my speech?

—Ready. Day after tomorrow the whole barrio will be in tears over your past and the unfortunate events of your childhood and we'll end with your little promises about an economic plan and the favor the president owes you. Smile, smile, a virile smile, here come the cameras.

One champion followed by another. But this one throws his punches in the ring. What corpulence! What muscles! What a fine, strong torso! Our Billy Carrasquillo, the feather weight champion, but his punch feels like iron. Watch him as he boxes alone, he's a true performance piece. Let's see . . . and what is Billy showing us? Ah . . . it's a telephone to remind us that it's time to get in touch with AT&E, the bridge between two cultures. Reach out and stay in touch, in touch, in touch with the enchanted island, with mama, papa, grandpa, the grandkids, that loved one, because there's so much to talk about ladies and gentlemen and young ladies here present and AT&E offers a 50% discount so you can talk all you want; and now you don't have to go to

Puerto Rico because you've got a friend in AT&E. Go ahead and talk, ladies, because there is so much to tell . . .

—Listen, yesterday I called up mami and it seems that things are getting hot.

—And what did she tell you?

—They caught Mari in Bayamón sniffing glue, but the worst thing was that she had already been cheating on her husband to pay for her habit, and they say that she's become a prostitute, but I don't know, I'm only telling you what they told me because when they caught her she was really high and they got her sister mixed up in the situation, I don't know if she sold it or distributed it, in any case the police also picked her up, but the whole mess really got worse when they found out that even her faggot brother had been sniffing it, and now they say he's got AIDS. I don't know, I'm telling you because it's so red hot.

This parade could not end without eating some delicious McDonald's burgers because Big Mac says WELCOME TO EAT HAMBURGERS. WELCOME PUERTO RICANS TO YOUR FAVORITE HAMBURGER, ALWAYS WELL-ACCOMPANIED BY A TASTY PEPSI; YOU KNOW, IT'S THE PEPSI GENERATION; and who can better illustrate this than the Mexican charro galloping on his mountain steed while holding a big, bubbly drink. And in the breeze he raises our one-starred flag, pues viva Puerto Rico no más, ándele pues. There's nothing more important in life than to be part of the Pepsi generation and yes, this is living and everything else is a tall tale.

Esteemed public this grand event closes with nothing less than a clown, what a nice touch of originality and great sense of humor on the part of the organizing committee. Yes sir, a clown.

What a delight! What charm! And dressed in the Puerto Rican flag. What a gas, really comical! He's plastered the star on his nose, the red and white stripes bleed together into multicolored dimensions. Where does each one end and the other begin?

—Listen, if that's not my homeboy . . . until last night he was in the slammer for raping his little sister.

—Remember how he put a tattoo of the flag on his ass?

Now there are thousands and thousands of flags marching behind this marvelous clown, thousands of flags my much esteemed public, covering the ground of this our second homeland. What do I hear in the distance? The sound of the guiro, the congas resound, the salsa has taken over the parade.

—Don't screw around brother, viva Puerto Rico, bro; tomorrow for sure I'm going to Borinquen—viva Puerto Rico.

Here everything is wild partying and joy in this glorious finale, I tell you that the New York Times will give us the best review ever, here was all the best of our people: such beauty, such culture, what a nation, what a show, yes sir! Yes sir!

ROMANTIC DISGRACE

She entered with her mane disheveled. It seemed as if a hurricane had just danced through it. She muttered under her breath because she had waited five minutes for the damned bus, which always ran late at the most important times of her life. Those were five long minutes of anguish, and to top it off, without the correct change needed to board this vehicle of her disgrace. She always forgot to pick up the seventy cents from the dresser her grandmother had bought at the second hand store. How could this have happened again if each time she looked at that inherited piece of furniture she remembered how her grandmother had haggled over the price with the agitated salesman. Since then she always associated that dresser with meticulously counted money.

She bumped into everything on her way up the steps. She suddenly felt the weight of her enormity. There was no way she would be able to get through all these people. She was out of breath. Her armpits had become pools of earthy scents with a faint hint of au de toilet that had almost disappeared. Her forehead sweated more than ever. The drops of perspiration seemed like lead weights being born, trickling down her face, then stagnating. Her make-up ran and the pink tones were mixing with the red. Her sweat became rivers forging canals through the Chanel base that had cost a pretty penny. It had been a bad idea to tighten her girdle a little more this morning—all this for the sake of stupid vanity. Her belly rolls ached and she began to feel a pain in her back that could easily paralyze her.

The curse of the TV dinners was exacting its revenge. When she gulped down that first succulent dish, she was already on the verge of being unemployed. The guest psychologist on the four o'clock show explained it very well—that she ate impulsively to try to rid herself of all that sexual frustration, sex which was not consummated due to all the other frustrations caused by her parents who, after all, were the reason for her immense girth.—She needed to fill a void, an immense void that no food could ever hope to fill. Such an explanation, so well thought out by such an incredibly erudite person, seemed to her to be a mystical illumination that would forge the beginning of her new life.

Long live the tube and its miracles. She'd have to explore all the channels until she found the perfect solution; but in the meantime she'd have to eat. Anyway her double stomach would not permit her to live the dreams created by **MADEMOISELLE**. Her spare tires scared off any possible Romeos announced by PEPSI, the new generation. Meanwhile she barreled ahead as her immense body kept her from fitting on the infernal summer bus. Her disgrace grew when the idiot of a bus driver shouted several times.

—Fatso, pay your fare.

—Who has change?

—Lady it takes bills.

—No way! I worked hard to get this greenback, mopping the stinking floors of those bankrupt rich folks. Who has change? No one here eats or drinks? Where's the change they gave you at the store?

—Here lady, take this.

—No way! I don't want a handout. I work from sunrise to sunset. But since you insist . . .

She watched the seventy cents slide down, illuminated by the interior light of that coin-eater. It seemed such a waste that a machine should eat the edible.—With those 70 cents I could have bought a TV dinner like the new ones they're testing.

The biggest mountain had been scaled. Now it was a question of finding a window seat where she could air out her armpits and plan out her route. She concentrated on the task of steadying herself as she became airborne every time the driver hit one of the potholes in the road. It seemed as if he sought them out on purpose just to see her swimming in the air. She floated and lurched like an inflated astronaut executing athletic stunts. The goal was achieved with honors conferred by the cheers from her audience.

—Row harder, you're almost there.

—Swim, orca, swim.

—Here heaven awaits you.

—Holy Virgin, you've made it.

The seat she so desired awaited her with the decade's most poetic graffiti: BABY I LOVED YOU HERE, GIVE IT UP IT'S MINE, I ALREADY HAD PEDRO, HE WHO READS THIS CAN GO TO HELL. She arrived, but her wide buttocks would not fit in their sensually lettered perch. No matter how hard she tried, a meaty portion hung over the edge with no visible means of support. She sighed deeply with the immense relief of knowing she had reached the promised land.

Now it was a matter of getting up her nerve and starting a conversation with the man who had gallantly offered to pay her fare. She noticed that from the beginning of her odyssey he had watched her with interest, or at least with curiosity. The psychologist had already explained that, in fact, many men were interested in robust women. This would be her lucky afternoon. She prayed to Saint Anthony to give her tact and femininity.

—And . . . you, what do you do?—she asked while grabbing her enormous plastic bag filled with boxes of pre-prepared foods.

—I write, ma'am.

—And you make a living from that?

—I think not.

—Make up your mind; I'm not going to be on this infernal bus my whole life. Take advantage of the fact that I'm here by your side right now.

Now that a conversation had begun she decided to throw herself into a daring adventure. She had nothing to lose, save the possible dislike of a starving writer. She started by rubbing against him with her multidimensional thigh. No, the poor guy wasn't getting her erotic signals; it seemed like he was navigating in his writer's daydreams. She went on to the second tactic, to place her foot between his. Nothing. He didn't react to anything. Now tired of brushing up against him and playing footsy, she remembered that this was unimportant compared to what she had in mind before taking the bus. In a matter of minutes she would be at the store of her good fortune.

She reached her destination: the store with the non-stop bargains: BUY TODAY—PAY TOMORROW, BUY ONE—GET THE SECOND ONE FREE, HERE WE FINANCE YOU, HERE WE CARE ABOUT YOU, HERE WE GIVE YOU EVERYTHING YOU DESIRE. A smile came to her face as the end of her journey drew near. She tried several times to reach the cord to signal for a stop, but she would only lose her balance and the equilibrium of her airborne buttock. "Listen, why don't you reach it for me, for God's sake?" The scholar agreed to this last request. She waited until the bus came to a complete stop to start her descent, tickled pink. She left filled with hope, with a firm step, ready to conquer discounts and to discover specials that only she could find. Her exit was triumphant, filled with frivolous retorts of—I hate you so much and I hate you even more.

NIGHT ON THE TOWN

I look at myself in the mirror only to see an unrecognizable reflection. How could all that elaborated beauty have disappeared in the space of an evening? With the terror of the catastrophe, deep blue circles reveal themselves framing those startled bird eyes. The fine eye liner, the mascara, the blue eye shadow—everything has become a pool of dark colors where you can hardly make out the small, tearful eyes covered with little red veins ready to burst. My lower lip, discolored and dry, trembles rapidly like someone with chills in the dead of winter. I try biting it to pacify my crying, but the attempt is in vain, because sobbing bursts from my mouth in wailing I cannot contain.

In this hopeless anguish, I want to pull out my hair till I bleed; but I come to my senses, realizing that last night's voluminous hairstyle is now a tattered wig in my hands and my premature baldness sets off the faded line of my eyebrows, where the sweat has forged canals that reach my swollen cheeks. How is this shocking sight possible if last night I was the envy of all my girlfriends, the center of attention? And look at me now, more run down than the victim of any fire, earthquake, hurricane or all three combined, in pain, dragging myself to this infernal mirror where I reckon accounts with myself, with life, where I see this face which I refuse to look at and I deny feeling this body so recently cut and scarred, punched and beaten, as if death waited for me just around the corner.

Where am I, Maritza, the ever beautiful, the perfumed one, who owns the street corner and the night? I look for you in this damned mirror, but I can't find you. I remove the make up, but you're not there. I only see this scarecrow of a being, this shadow of shadows—not Maritza of the night. I search my memory until I remember the world I had constructed, this reality that we had created in order to survive.

It all started with our aesthetic routine, which made us beautiful, splendid, ready for a night on the town. When it was time to apply the make-up, we always had a blast, Lucy and me. She was blacker than the night, and she painted herself as if she were a white girl, with shades of pink as if for a debutant party. Logically I set her straight and told her to drop the inferiority complex; that we were going whoring, not to parade in Casa España. She played like she hadn't heard and continued applying her pink translucent eye shadow. She had delicately placed all the creams and powders on her vanity, with all the meticulousness of a professional cosmetologist, while she sang rancheras in the style of Rocío Durcal. After an arduous hour in front of the mirror, I was stunning, ready to pick up the first macho that crossed my path. But no, I had to recoup my patience and remove Lucy's false white mascara to transform here into an African goddess. She was truly all woman. In a matter of minutes, and with little make-up, the difference was immediately obvious.

—Damn you, you were born to be a woman. With this angel face and guitar-shaped body, no woman could ever compete with you. God's only mistake was your penis. And now even your race is in vogue—so don't complain!

—Ah girlfriend, but this color doesn't help me at all . . .

—Don't be a fool. Why do you want to be white? Let's see . . . if we white women wrinkle faster than a raisin and the first illness we catch makes us look like death warmed over. Calm down about this color thing, you're always the first to get picked up, so chill out, okay?

Those dresses we had seen in **ELLE** and later sewn for ourselves turned out perfect. My dear Lucy, you always dreamed of dressing like an innocent vampire and that black outfit hugged your curvy, guitar-shaped body like a second skin. What class, and what style you had in your walk. You seemed like a swan floating on a tranquil lake in some exotic country. That transparent blouse beautifully marked your breasts which we had so carefully designed. The skirt hugged the curves of your uplifted derriere and showed off those voluptuous hips that just screamed out to be caressed.

I, on the other hand, the unfortunate one, had not been blessed at birth with your body. My masculine bone structure gave me away at a distance, so I had to camouflage it with a lot of loose material so that the focus would always be directed toward my work of art, toward this woman's face skillfully painted with the finest of pencils.

Every eyebrow we painted, every accessory we put on, brought us closer to the so-admired sex. Our voices changed, we adjusted our diction perfectly and the feminine mannerisms came so naturally that no man could resist them. We looked at ourselves in the mirror, and without a doubt, we were firmly convinced that we were women: you, the exquisite magazine model and me, the impacting woman of cosmetics.

The taxi driver who picked us up on the corner didn't take his eye off the rearview mirror. He was devouring you with his eyes and you were as distant as always. Knowing that you possess a beauty that bewitches men, you did not even dignify him by giving him a glance. He wet his lips, he bit them, sighed . . . all this and without any of it registering in your gaze of untouchable goddess. When we got out he refused to accept his fare, and in that precise moment, like a well-planned stratagem, you blew him a kiss which the fool received as if it had come from heaven.

—Girlfriend, what the hell do you do to these men?

—Nothing my dear. I offer them lots of silence and mystery, creating an illusion: the fantasy that I am beautiful, but I'm not for them.

—And if they find you out . . .

—Men are fools and they're easily deceived.

When we entered the club the music was at full volume. The Cuban son had taken over the ambiance to give the place an extravagantly tropical feel. All those hips just couldn't be repressed. The soft rubbing of bodies incited the dance, now on fire. They danced close. Four entwined legs moved oh so slowly in the space of a single tile. The flute and the maracas kept the beat while the guiro rasped at the air. Their pores sweated, releasing fragrances of fashionable perfumes mixed with the preliminary aroma of sex, detectable by a good sense of smell. This simmering water made itself felt in the laughter and in those moist lips that covered their partners with kisses. This was not a place to just observe; here one lived the intensity of the moment. The desperate desire to manifest themselves in body and soul was the order of the day. And you were so calm, as if you weren't included in this nocturnal lust, as if it weren't happening right there beside you.

That real handsome guy, Mario, had been checking you out since we made our entrance. For the last couple of months that clever fox had been trying to lasso you and you kept on as indifferent as always. His sleepy blue eyes drove your competitors wild, the poor things sighed like foolish adolescents when they saw him pass. This wise guy knew how to caress his wavy blonde hair, give a half turn, flex his muscles and continue his strut down the runway exhibiting his Armani-style Italian suit; all this showing off, just for his Lucy. The poor guy was so stuck on his African goddess that he would say such sweet things like "cu cu ca chu, ah my love, I'm already feeling you o—." But all this bored you so much that I could tell by looking at your face that you wanted to exit, running. Here no one played the game you were looking for. Guessing and guessing again to see if you know who you will go to bed with.

—Let's get out of here; I'm fed up with this place.

—But darling, what's the matter? We barely got here.

—Woman, this bores me, here everyone knows what we are. There's no intrigue, no mystery. These are just a bunch of semi-machos that want to believe the illusion that they are going to bed with a woman, but they know very well that we have that thing that gives us away. In this place no one has seduced anyone. Let's meet some real men that really believe this fantasy that we've created. After they've sampled a bit, they won't turn back.

We always ended up like this, with your game, your desire to be accepted for what, deep down, you were not. Because you had already convinced yourself you had changed, that you lived in another body, in this fantasy of the created physiognomy. I was always the insecure one, the one easy to please, the phobic one; so to earn your respect I'd follow you to the bottom of the abyss until we'd found the reason for our pilgrimage that night.

We left the club and began to swivel our hips. We took six or seven steps when one of your admirers stopped in front of us, the taxi driver, the one who devoured your glance. The chauffeur had found a friend who wasn't at all bad and now they invited us to get in the cab. For you this was your greatest fantasy, to make love to a taxi driver that courted you as if you were an irresistible woman. Logically he had been waiting for you; this guy had read well that sign you had given him when you threw him that airborne kiss. He had waited and now you had landed here with your sideways glance. These people don't mess around: they tell you exactly what they think, without any pretense, without the least consideration for the fact that they are addressing a couple of ladies.

—Sweet *mamacita*, precious, how about a ride in the park? Look the night is young and full of fun. Don't give me that offended look. I'm the one who's suffering, because I smell cinnamon but I can't get none.

—Maritza, it looks like this taxi driver has a tongue and speaks, but in the taxi he didn't say a peep.

—Not only do I have a tongue, but I know how to use it to please you my queen.

—And how do you know what I like?

—Let's see, get in, my beauty, and I'll find out.

The man was right on target when he said "I'll find out," because this was precisely your world, to cover and uncover, to pleasure with your surprise or to provoke terror with the truth. To continue your little game, this was the plan, because after all life is a card game and we were experts. Your desire to get in was immediately noticeable. You started stroking the handle delicately as if tempted by the idea until at last you pulled on the latch and we climbed in. The taxi driver knew the area like the back of his hand and in less than half an hour we were in one of the most remote parks of the city. Everything was covered in darkness and a silence that would have scared the dead. He parked the car among some bushes, and almost in unison, both of them threw themselves on us with a ravenous appetite.

How well we knew the story, they wanted to go directly to the heart of the action, to the crevice of feminine delight, but this would give us away, it would put an end to our secret game. Since we had already been giving ourselves hormone injections for three months, there were many pleasures we could offer before they discovered our secret. The plan was always the same, to guide them slowly down the erotic path, step by step, culminating in total submission, if it were accepted. The long, deep kisses, the passionate caresses, were the preamble that would lead them to forcefully suck those delicate breasts.

The taxi driver and his friend rose to the occasion, they let themselves be led by our skilled hands that guided them, like blind men; now there was no rush, but they were getting increasingly excited. Little by little they undressed us while they nibbled, kissed, squeezed our bodies so femininely offered. I noticed that Lucy was speeding up; something had taken her off her studied path. Her companion was all worked up, firmly placing his erect member between her legs, demanding immediate action. To get out of that fix she knelt before him, took out his hot, enormous rod and began to suck it to pacify the driver's demands.

The situation began to worsen. While the driver let himself be pleasured, I noted how he insistently searched for Lucy's vulva. She would evade his groping, looking for a way around his encountering what he so longed for. That night my girlfriend had hermetically wrapped her cargo of manhood with adhesive tape. She carried her little masculine package between her legs, tightly plastered against her skin so that it was nothing more than a slight bulge to the touch.

Lucy did not count on her man's sudden, unexpected show of strength. In a matter of seconds he put her in an arm lock and proceeded to open her legs by interposing his own. When she was completely exposed, he searched with desperation for the opening that she had insistently denied him. When his enormous penis bumped into the little package taped to the skin of his battle prize, the expression on his face changed. He glared in consternation and with brutal force he yanked off the tape, exposing my girlfriend's dangling genitals in the air.

Without giving her time to prepare herself, he began to punch her in the face, drawing blood from her eyes and mouth while he shouted non-stop—"Shit-faced faggot, you're gonna pay for this with your life."—When he tired of hitting her, he took a knife from the glove compartment and with renewed anger he buried the blade in her chest repeatedly until she let out her last scream for mercy. All this happened like a flash of lightning. I had remained paralyzed, immobile, without knowing what to do in the face of such unexpected horror.

I was still there and the driver's friend felt obliged to show his machismo and camaraderie with his dishonored buddy. He whispered in my ear—"I don't have any choice, baby"—and he told me this because we had felt each other; he knew full well what he'd gotten himself into and he was willing to go all the way if it hadn't been for the disapproval of his friend. He had to prove himself; it was the law of life. He took brass knuckles from his pocket and he began to punch me in the stomach, slowly working his way up until he got to my face, like slow torture that had to deform that which had so easily seduced him. In his eyes I detected a sadness that did not go with the beating he'd unleashed against my body. Our situation had been different. In the silence of our caresses we had exposed our truths, his taste for what he knew as taboo . . . but he still wanted it. My screams, cries, and the blood I'd spilled helped to convince the driver of his friend's manhood.

—We should leave them in the middle of the highway so the traffic finishes them off—proposed the taxi driver.

—We'd better leave this one here so we don't cause any suspicion.

I look at myself in this mirror and I can still see the cars running over your body. All the life gone out of you, the cars' bumpers tossed you from one side of the highway to the other like a deflated ball, without the least attempt to stop to pick up the human carcass that rolled on the asphalt. When I recuperated from passing out, your cadaver had disappeared; I don't know whether it rolled away or if some soul had taken pity on that horrible spectacle.

I try to remove the make-up that has become encrusted in my wounds, but I only succeed in causing more pain to this already deformed skin. This infernal mirror is the assassin of my soul. It keeps reminding me of the deformation of my face, of the memory of some invented beauty. I keep looking for you in the reflection, my dear Lucy, but the coordinates of your eyes escape me and I only hear this noisy box announcing your death, your defeat in life—"homosexual transvestite dies run over by an automobile"—is all I hear. I look at myself in the mirror to pierce this nothingness which I cannot see and I remain fragmented, broken in a thousand pieces, searching for the remnants so that I might construct your gaze.

THE SWARM

The longing to become one entangled in the sheets looking for the entrance of pleasure dominating ecstasy with a single word itself multiplying in syllables of sweat accentuating the languid body that dies with each exit with no time for pardoning because forgiveness is non-existent in this act of love which is not love but something beyond pleasure that grinds itself into every inch of skin in each mouth nourished on its own flavor augmenting the heat of each sigh of every moan of each groan of bliss in the drunkenness of what is called lascivious libido to feel surrendered to all agony to each stumbling step taken because to drink the other's air is to come alive living in this thing called the potency of the body that wants to feel what it has yet to discover in the blood that accumulates in the glass that extends itself strengthening every vein every path of this forced transit with no outlet and at the distance yet so near so tight so tied up in itself demanding liberation inviting the foreign kiss the kiss that swarms between the softness of the touch and the abrupt rupture of that denied and desired smallness because it is not denied but postponed everything desired in this lucid madness electrifies the senses confuses the intellect and carries on until the no more love because I want more than what I have known because in every demand one discovers that this circle of arms extended and freely given was never begun to this your strength wanting to arrive wanting to deposit all your unbridled passion which you can no longer amass because you have liberated yourself you have seen that this longing to become one is to multiply oneself.

A STORY TO BE SUNG

el prefigurado*

You tend to make your morning visits while the birds still sing, when the aroma of coffee fills the air; and handsomely you recline like that, nude, ardent, with your virile strength exposed as if imposing a ring of happiness, of a joy that only you know. Prefigurado, when you make your morning visits and take your time theorizing on love, in every caress, in each palpitation of my body, which is your body in invention, because we well know that you do not exist, that solitary you arrive to impress your footprint in the depths, to leave the taste of your being to birds that still sing in the night.

beginning

I know that when you look at me with your green eyes of summer, your skin begins to burn, weaving itself into a bronze statue. In praise of your being, strength of taut, assonant muscles that pursue this dark Antilles glance that creeps into your eyes through this green sea you call a gaze. And to know you on a fiery night, when the Jamaican steel drums clamor and

---

* the anticipated one

resonate with the rhythms of calypso and limbo, is to decipher the enigma that makes you a man, imagining the salty spray of sweat that permeates your body; today, the day of our meeting, acknowledging the beginning of our love. How could I know it was you, the prefigured one, the man that must be *the man*?

angela's cafe

Here our love is about to be born. With this, your first sip of coffee, your lips nearing the cup as if anticipating a kiss. We look at each other with a centuries-old fear, because men should not want each other with the intensity and audacity that we do. We make a braid with the words that define us, discovering that in every flight each encounters the other. Your smile filters through my pores and again I feel this visage of the green sea. Where are you taking me with your clear eyes? What is the contour of your being? How can one decipher the memorable first encounter? Our hands touch beneath the table, revealing the secret, discovering the lie, because men should not love this way, with the boldness that we do.

long walks

Our footsteps carry us to these beautiful mangroves where the caimans hide in the shade of a tree. They slink down to the dark waters where their vertebrae appear for a brief moment. In the same way, you begin to discover my greatest fears, the phobias of a Caribbean who has never seen such enormous amphibians. You tell me that you have swum in their waters, that it's a matter of getting accustomed to the idea, that all things are equal: animal, water, life and death. I admire this strange sense of valor, embracing that which is already one. Boy who is man. Man who is boy. The afternoon unfolds, salty, in a lazy mood. We've reached the palm grove and the sands that unite my island with your peninsula. In the distance, the crawfish horizon swallows us with its orange mouth, expanding from its bowels to reveal the monster with blue, painted claws. And we begin imagining with this transforming sunset what it would be like to touch each others' hands, feeling them palpable, tactile, full of uncontainable strength where the desire of censored love is deposited. Because our affection will not be public, but at the borders of our imagination, where things silent persist in proclaiming our love. Here the leaves accumulate along our path. Exploring them we discover a time not our own, somewhat diluted by the passing minutes, imprecise hours, stagnant hours. These long walks led me to know your life, a labyrinth of lights that have enclosed the air, the wind that defines existence.

CUESTIÓN DE HOMBRES

BENITO PASTORIZA IYODO

CUESTIÓN DE HOMBRES

Mi padre siempre sonreía a solas. Difícil era que se le dibujara una sonrisa en esa cara tosca de guajiro cubano. Mamá se enfurecía cuando lo descubría riéndose ante el espejo como si en ese momento su imagen le estuviese haciendo el chiste del año. Ella que nunca le sacaba un movimiento de los labios no comprendía aquel ritual de soledad y alegría que disfrutaba papá. La felicidad la llevaba por dentro, como quien disfruta algo a hurtadillas sin que el resto del mundo se entere.

Por esos días cuando cumplía yo los ocho años le dio con mirarme con una extraña sonrisa como si intentara incluirme en la maravilla de su mundo. Al principio pensé que mi padre comenzaba a verse en mí, la continuación de su prole, el reflejo niño de su ser. La duplicación de su vida que en alguna forma vendría a darse en mí, en ese niño al que se lo permitía todo, sin un regaño, sin un escarmiento. Porque para él la vida se sumaba en lo breve y el hijo llegaba para disfrutar intensamente el momento fugaz del existir.

Papá que murió a los siete años en Pinar del Río, ciudad costera al noroeste de La Habana, resucitó a los nueve días después de una ardua lucha entre la vida y la muerte. Los santeros de conchas y piedras lo trajeron del submundo marino donde su alma había ido a descansar. Abuela que parió once niñas en busca del varón, viró tierra y mar para que le regresaran el macho de su estirpe.

Cuando papá dio el segundo suspiro de su vida, abuela le prometió a Santa Bárbara bendita jamás separarse de su hijo. Hasta los dieciocho años estuvo durmiendo papá con abuela y abuelo. Por la noche cuando estiraba sus piernas podía sentir el roce encendido de sus cuerpos, el suave gemido de ella que pedía prontitud del acto por la presencia del niño. El niño ya se venía aprendiendo los embelecos del amor.

La extraña sonrisa de papá comenzó a seguirme por todas partes. El baño, lugar de mi ritual para el aseo, lo rondaba como en busca de un secreto, de algo que yo guardaba que él discretamente habría de descubrir. Las visitas al baño se hicieron más esporádicas e imprevistas para que papá no se enterara de mis callados gemidos, de las lágrimas que me bebía por el insoportable dolor que me salía de entre las piernas. Algo se imaginaba, algo se descifraba en la sonrisa cómplice de mi padre.

Mamá en cambio siempre fue más directa en su acercamiento. Las sutilezas no eran parte de su envergadura emocional. Nos recordaba siempre que había nacido en la noche de San Ciprián y que ese terrible huracán que devastó la isla, se le había quedado por dentro por el resto de sus días. Todo lo calculaba, lo medía, lo tasaba. De ella no se escapaban los olores y los sabores. Todo quedaba escudriñado, examinado, vertido y revertido. Fue hija de comerciantes y no perdía el tiempo con regodeos, "Al pan pan y al vino vino"—decía ella cuando quería hablar bien claro, "y tú, ¿por qué pasas tanto tiempo en el baño y por qué te ha dado ahora con lavar los calzoncillos?"

La respuesta fue un rotundo silencio.

Días después los dos amanecieron con la misma sonrisa. La sonrisa inviolable, la que no se permitía ser descifrada. Mi padre de poco hablar y mucho decir se acercó y me susurró al oído, "hijo a veces hay que hacerse hombre y no siempre es cuando se quiere." Las palabras sonaron a sentencia. Habían descubierto el secreto, la íntima agonía de mi sufrimiento estaba expuesta sin que supiese yo adonde me llevaría.

El día que me tocó morir jugaba damas con mi hermana. Ella con un deseo obvio de dejarse ganar no convencía en su actuación. Siempre reñíamos por cada movida, acusándonos de trampas inventadas en nuestra loca imaginación, todo para construir el ardid de la victoria. Ese día noté que por contagio o pena llevaba la misma sonrisa de mis padres. Evitaba la discusión y se comportaba de una manera exageradamente bondadosa. El silencio aprendido de mi padre no me permitía hacerle la pregunta, a ella la que todo lo sabía, la que para todo tenía una respuesta. La curiosidad ganó la partida y me envalentoné.

—¿Me va a doler?

—¿Qué cosa te va a doler?

—¿Me va a doler la muerte?

—Papá nunca me contó si le dolió o no.

—¿Seré el mismo?

—Dicen que después de la muerte naces hombre, no sé.

—¿Y de qué moriré?

—Vas a morir de lo que morimos todos, morirás de la muerte.

Nunca comprendí por qué me vistieron de domingo para conocer la muerte. Mamá se regocijaba verme vestido de blanco. Una alegría se le apoderaba del cuerpo y me vestía con el afán de como quien va a ver el Papa. Los pantalones cortos que tanto odiaba los combinaba con una camisa de hilo blanco que remataba con unos zapatos del mismo color. Lo mejor del ritual era llegar a usar la colonia de papá, oler a él era un privilegio que se daba en muy pocas y contadas ocasiones. "Ese es mi macho," solía decir después de vestirme con todo el esmero como una de las muñecas de mi hermana.

Papá con una mano muy firme se agarró de la mía y con una voz que parecía venir de muy lejos me dijo "vámonos a hacernos hombres." La tosquedad guajira le regresó a su rostro y la sonrisa que tanto me intrigaba desapareció. En el transcurso del viaje no me dirigió la palabra y parecía que iba tragando nudos de acero.

Al llegar, esperamos pacientemente en una sala donde entraba y salía gente con unas caras muy tristes. Noté que algunas personas que iban de blanco como yo me miraban con curiosidad, acaso complicidad. Una de ellas se acercó a nosotros y muy solemnemente nos dijo "el señor doctor está listo para él." Papá me apretó la mano más fuerte que nunca, al punto de casi lastimarme.

Todo fue tan rápido y tan lento. Las señoras en blanco comenzaron a desvestirme mientras el señor doctor se ponía unas telas que le cubrían el rostro. Otro se acercó con un plato cubierto de tijeritas y extraños cuchillos. Comencé a llorar. Ya desnudo me treparon sobre una mesa metálica fría donde me abrieron las piernas de par en par, que fueron amarradas con unas correas para asegurarse de que no me fuera a mover. Escuché cuando el señor de la máscara le dijo a papá "esto es cuestión de rutina y se hace despierto." Mis gritos comenzaron a zumbar por las cuatro esquinas. "Te odio papá, te odio papá."

El primer corte fue el más que dolió. Mis lágrimas y mis gritos no daban abasto para expresar el dolor y la humillación que sentía. Escupía al doctor mientras éste cortaba y cortaba sin parar mis adentros. Cada corte profundizaba más en el dolor.

Papá sudaba y se mordía los labios mientras yo le gritaba a todo pulmón—"papá sácame de aquí, seré bueno, seré bueno."

El viaje al infierno no terminaba. El tiempo se quedó estancado en aquel cuarto. Cuando escuché al doctor decir—aguja—el mundo se quebrantó en millones de pedazos. Mi cuerpo mojado en sudor ya no encontraba lágrimas o gritos que aplacaran el dolor. Ya rendido ante el desgaste sólo podía llorar sin cesar mientras aquella aguja perforaba la piel ensangrentada.

La pesadilla de conocer la muerte terminó con un baño. Las mujeres en blanco invadieron mis adentros con un alcohol que quemaba lo más recóndito de mi debilitado cuerpo. Me vistieron en el traje blanco de domingo y fui instruido a que caminara con las piernas bien abiertas para que no sintiera el dolor post-operatorio. "A éste se lo pueden llevar. Ya podrá hacer familia y gozar la vida. Me lo traen al mes para cortarle los puntos."

Gozar la vida. Mi padre me cargó entre sus brazos con el cuidado de una paloma herida. Comencé a sangrar levemente. Una fina línea roja se iba marcando en los pantalones blancos. Gozar la vida. El goteo rojo comenzó a humedecer el brazo de mi padre. Observé como su frente sudaba, los ojos iban estancados en un gran pozo de agua. Gozar la vida. Los brazos le temblaban de una forma extraña. Apenas llevaba bien el paso. Yo, sumido en el dolor, sentía que algo se desvanecía, algo se moría por dentro. Intenté buscar la sonrisa cómplice de mi padre que habría de incluirme en la maravilla de su mundo, en el placer prometido de hacerme hombre, de sentir la enorme puerta que se abriría ante la vida.

LA BASURA

El día que llovió basura acabábamos de llegar de Puerto Rico. Mami como siempre encantada de comenzar sus nuevos negocios, ya que representarían regresar a la isla después de arduos años de trabajo. Se fijó una meta clara, "Nene, después de que trabaje y trabaje duro, en menos de tres años estamos de vuelta." Parecía tener que justificarse constantemente al tener que repetirle la misma frase a mi hermana, pero con una variante, "Nena no te preocupes, no llores, que esto no es para largo." Mi hermana venía llorando desde el avión y hasta gritos se le salieron, "¡Lo odio, lo odio, lo odio con todas mis fuerzas!"

Mi padre que no se atrevía a mirarnos, se encerró en su culpa y por los años restantes no nos volvió a mirar a los ojos. Siempre tuvo debilidad por las mujeres. Desde Cuba ya lo apodaban el pony cerrero porque se pasaba saltando de yegua en yegua. Él con todo su orgullo de macho guapo se jactaba de todas las conquistas logradas durante la época de su soltería. Le costó sentar cabeza los primeros años del matrimonio y después . . . a cabalgar nuevamente. La última en la cabalgata se llamó Lydia. La bien querida conocía perfectamente las artes de la seducción y había logrado domesticar al pony, al punto de sacarle el último centavo que poseía la familia.

El entusiasmo no le permitió a mi madre ver el lugar a donde habíamos llegado. Era un edificio decrépito en una calle colmada de drogadictos y traficantes armados hasta los dientes. Las puertecillas de los buzones habían sido forzadas dejando al descubierto cualquier cheque del welfare que llegase. Eso explicaba porque cada lunes se reunían todas las welferianas a la entrada del edificio esperando al amado Don Wilfre, como solían llamarle al que bien las mantenía. El pasillo era un largo túnel hediondo a orín, alumbrado en el centro por una pequeña bombilla que prestaba luz sobre la pequeña circunferencia del mismo. Al entrar en ese túnel del tiempo se volvía actor la posible víctima. Se corría desde la entrada hasta el halo de luz, ya debajo de éste no se divisaba nada a los lados, era estar en escenario, cegado por la luz y expuesto por la oscuridad. La puerta al apartamento era una gran construcción de latón a prueba de ladrones.

El apartamento era mágico. Al entrar en él todo se llenaba de luz a causa de las grandes ventanas halladas en los tres cuartos. El cuarto central era cocina comedor bañera. Nos divertía saber que bastaba con quitar la enorme tapa que cubría la bañera y ésta se transformaba de mesa a fuente de aseo. Comíamos y nos bañábamos en el mismo cuarto y desde allí podíamos saltar a nuestro dormitorio para ver a Batman o a la sala recámara de mis padres para ver la basura llover. Desde las enormes ventanas divisábamos el pequeño patio que con apenas seis pies de profundidad se sumía debajo de nuestro balcón. El patio estaba lleno de basura y faltaban algunos tres pies para que nos alcanzara. Era como ver una piscina llenarse, no de agua, de basura.

El uso primario y principal del balcón era por si ocurría un incendio, pero nuestros vecinos gustaban de solearse, volar chiringas, tomarse sus cervezas y de vez en cuando hacer el amor. Preferían las horas nocturnas cuando ellos pensaban que ya todos dormían. Claro que se enteraba todo el vecindario de los shows en carne viva, especialmente cuando los protagonistas se daban por gritar y gemir como si estuvieran en sus propias camas. Al ocurrir esto les tiraban baldes de agua fría y rápidamente se les bajaba el calentón.

Nuestros vecinos llevaban una vida agitada. Desde sus balcones llovían condones, agujas ensangrentadas, latas, pepsi cola, kotex, pampers reusados, cajas de cherrios, bolitas de sangre en bolsa, carne guisada, pasteles, arroz con pollo, productos Goya, Don Q, discos de Daniel Santos, de La Lupe, Olga Guillot, cartas de amor, TV dinners, lechuga, tomate, aguacate, poemas, lápices, fotografías de personas extrañas, revistas de gente desnuda en posiciones extrañas, cigarrillos, ceniceros, Colgate, peinillas, hair spray, jabón, jamón, cartón, salchichón, perros, gatos, pajaritos, Buen Hogar, Vanidades, juguetes, muñecas, penes plásticos, saliva, salsa, ajo, cebolla, perejil, queso, cucarachas y muchas ratas, muchas ratas vivas nadando en ese mar de basura. Muchas veces adivinábamos lo que hacían por lo que llovía. Cáscaras de huevos, lata Carnation, azúcar—cocinaban flan. Fotografías, cigarrillos, botellas—comenzaba la pelea.

No nos gustó nada el día que a nuestros padres se les ocurrió la horrible idea de que era el momento de iniciarse en las clases. Eso representaba tener que instruirse en inglés, lengua que desconocíamos por completo. El primer día fue una tortura. Escuchamos a la profesora de inglés hablar de un tal Othello, que si era negro igual que nosotros los puertorriqueños y demás negros de la clase, que el pobrecito no sabía que quería de la vida y la clase alzada tirándole papeles, tizas y borradores a la muy blanca maestra.

El maestro de español era un chino que le costaba un enorme trabajo pronunciar nuestros apellidos llenos de eres. Ese día se empeñó en enseñarnos el abecedario y no logramos convencerle que eso ya lo habíamos aprendido muchos años atrás. Después de las clases básicas nos mandaron a los respectivos talleres de acuerdo a nuestras nacionalidades, los asiáticos a los laboratorios, los negros a mecánica y los puertorriqueños a carpintería. Pasé tres horas aprendiendo como hacer un colgador de corbatas. Al regalárselo a mi padre, me miró con una curiosidad sonriente, no se explicaba como lograron sacar de mí, un comelibros, aquel artefacto tan inservible.

Saliendo de la escuela en ese nuestro primer día, mi hermana notó que un hombre nos seguía. Apresuramos el paso y desviándonos de nuestra ruta, logramos desaparecer de su vista. Al llegar a nuestro edificio una de las señoras welferianas esperaba pacientemente al cartero. Eso de algún modo alivió nuestro miedo. Ya listos para entrar al pasillo que conocíamos como el túnel del tiempo, "entras hoy pero no sales mañana," la señora se apresuró a detenernos, "no entren que hay un tipo que lleva un rato metido en el pasillo, no sé si se la está inyectando o esperándolos a ustedes." Efectivamente, al describirnos el tipo, resultó ser el mismo que nos venía siguiendo. Mi hermana que ya estaba metida en la pubertad, le entró el pánico de que la cosa sería con ella. No pudimos disuadirla y por poco comienza sus bien conocidos ataques de llantos.

Ya oscurecía cuando nuestra protectora se decidió entrar sola al pasillo. Quería asegurarse que aquello andaba sin peligro. Salió con una sonrisa no muy convincente, "parece que ése se fue por el rufo, porque no se le ve ni en pintura." Un poco calmados llegamos hasta la puerta en compañía de la señora y abriendo los cuatro candados, entramos a la magia del apartamento que creíamos seguro. Ella se despidió con la sonrisa ya borrada, nosotros se lo achacamos al cansancio de tener que esperar tanto tiempo con nosotros afuera.

Al entrar escuchamos unos ruidos, pero rápidamente nos acordamos que aquí llovía basura y que debían ser unas latas cayendo en el patio. De tanto nerviosismo no encontrábamos el interruptor de luz. Cuando por fin dimos con él, la luz nos hizo ver un piso blanco salpicado de ratas corriendo como locas por todas partes. Nuestro primer instinto fue treparnos sobre la mesa bañera y mirar con horror aquel espectáculo. Mi hermana me señaló que mirara hacia la ventana y efectivamente la basura ya había alcanzado nuestro balcón.

Ahora éramos parte de todo este desperdicio. A nuestro alrededor se acumulaba la inmundicia ajena, botellas, excremento, plástico, lodazal, carne podrida, cristales rotos, y un mar de objetos que habían perdido forma y sentido. Entre la basura que colgaba del balcón, logramos ver unas largas piernas que se contraían en fuerza tratando de abrir la enorme ventana que apenas nos separaba del basurero. Reconocimos la cara de aquél que nos había perseguido. Mi hermana me miró desesperadamente como si su vida terminase allí. En su mirada vi el terror del que será asediado por una invasión extraña. Aquella pesadilla enmudeció el aire y sólo se escuchaba los gemidos de mi hermana en aumento, su ahogada voz en llanto que en letanía morbosa gritaba, “lo odio, lo odio, lo odio.”

LA BOLSA DEL PLACER

Cuando me despierto en la noche puedo ver desde mi oscuro rincón las enormes ratas nadando en el lapachero. Al principio me causaron pavor porque me recordaron de la vez que sentimos sus miles de piecitos sobre nuestros cuerpos. Aquello nos pasó por lo del cumpleaños de la rechonchita. Esa idea de Pachín de ponernos a espiar las fiestas que prometen.

Llevábamos todo el día buscando comida en los basureros hasta que por fin dimos con un familión celebrando un pasadía con harta comida. Los platos se desbordaban con tacos, enchiladas, ensaladas, carnes, frijoles y cantidad sobrada de tortillas. Supimos de inmediato que allí la comida sobraría, que las bolsas plásticas se llenarían de esa comida familiar tan gustosa. Sería cuestión de esperar. Le cantaron las mañanitas a la niña gordita con cachetes color melón y vimos el pastel rosado colmado de fresas y crema, coronado con una muñequita plástica que se parecía a la niña. Ese día nos pondríamos las botas.

Al rato la piñata explotó después que un niño fuertote y grandotote le dio tremendo golpe al burrito de papel azul y a la niña que se encontraba cerca. La niña lloraba a todo pulmón mientras los demás niños corrían como locos a buscar sus dulces. Nosotros íbamos ubicando aquellos dulces que rebotaban lejos de las miradas feroces para luego recogerlos de los lugares precisos en donde habían caído. Nuestras tripas iban dando tumbos cuando por fin se decidió el familión despedirse de las amistades y los invitados.

La despedida duró casi más que la fiesta, por lo menos así lo sentían los relojes de nuestros estómagos. Nuestra alegría se colmó cuando vimos que Doña Limpieza, toda fiesta tiene una, tiraba los platos de papel con la comida intacta a la bolsa, no los vació en otra bolsa ni nada por el estilo. La comida estaría servida, sería cuestión de sacarla de la bolsa y a comer se ha dicho. Al irse la familia, sacamos con cuidado tres o cuatro platos y empezamos a saborear aquellas sobras que tan bien sabían después de días sin comer.

Sobró bastante comida y fue idea del Pachín de llevárnosla esa misma noche al túnel. Tuvimos que aguardar que los otros se fueran, cosa que no dieran con el tesoro que habíamos encontrado, comida para por lo menos tres días. Ya para entonces conocía yo las ratas, pero de lejos, había aprendido a esquivarlas, buscarles la vuelta, sin meterme demasiado en este mundo subterráneo que también les pertenecía. Pachín pensó que el mejor lugar para cuidar la comida sería tenerla de cabecera, cosa que si se acercaban los otros ya los podríamos atrapar. Así fue como nos recostamos y colocamos la bolsa casi sobre nuestras cabezas.

La noche ya estaba entrada y las panzas llenas y por lo tanto nos entró el maldito sueño. Eso de dormir no conviene en este mundo. Cuando nos dormíamos en el otro alcantarillado siempre nos pasaba algo que nos acercaba más a la muerte. En el alcantarillado de los Coyotes a Pachín se le ocurrió dormirse y nos dieron tremenda paliza los que de allí se habían adueñado. Estuvimos sangrando un par de días y a mí no me cicatrizaba la cara. El tajo que me habían dado me cubría medio cachete y parecía una de esas medias lunas que se aparecen en las noches donde todo está a medio iluminar.

No entrado bien el sueño comencé a sentir un cosquilleo en la planta del pie. No le presté atención pensando que nuevamente sería Pachín con una de sus sandeces y cerré los ojos para que aquel sueño indebido llegara. Luego sentí un bulto pesado plantarse en las nalgas. Desde allí comenzó a emitir sonidos extraños como si estuviera comunicándose con una tropa. Aquel acto me paralizó, intenté moverme y el pánico no me permitía respirar. Pensé en la última paliza que nos habían dado, en mi cara cortada, en las muchas que serían. El Pachín dormía a pata estirá. No había manera de saber cuántas ratas se encontraban sobre su cuerpo. De soslayo pude ver una rata que le escarbaba la nariz. Los dientes afilados se engomaban con lo que sacaba de los orificios nasales de Pachín. No lograba sacar voz de mi garganta, ni un grito, ni un aullido. Me espantaba de mi espanto.

Ahora sentía unas quince ratas subiendo y bajando por el costado de mi espalda. La bolsa ya había sido rota y de ella sustraían el tesoro de la fiesta que habíamos espiado. Sentía sus pezuñas rasgar mi cara, entrar en la piel del cuero cabelludo. Mi cuerpo inmóvil se había vuelto la carretera hacia su alimento. Algunas eran tan largas y gordas que apenas podían con su cuerpo y se sentía la lentitud con que llevaban su peso hacia la bolsa. Y Pachín muerto en su sueño, roncando como si aquello no estuviese pasando. Su boca abierta por el ronquido, era parada necesaria para las que por allí pasaban. Intenté gritar pero el miedo paralizaba todo intento de poder salvarme.

Ya había visto una niña en el túnel morir de rabia. La chamaca la mordió una rata el primer día que entró al alcantarillado. Había huido de su familia porque quedó preñada de uno de los chamacos del barrio. No pudo bregar con la vergüenza de ser señalada y se metió aquí con nosotros. Al principio se le vio muy valentona, pero horas después la pobre tiritaba de miedo y frío como si la hubieran transportado al peor de sus sueños. Su cuerpo se rindió rápidamente a la enfermedad y a los pocos días la agarró la muerte con su pancita de madre que se le notaba ya.

Aquel rostro en agonía se pintaba en mi memoria mientras las patitas de las ratas corrían rápidamente sobre mi espalda. Pachín, despierta, Pachín, me repetía en el silencio de la mente. Al parecer todo el sueño del mundo se empozó sobre mi cuate, cuando noté que éste abrió un ojo y me guiñó una señal de alerta. Ya teníamos nuestras señales secretas y ésta significaba a correr como locos cueste lo que cueste. A la segunda guiñada saltamos como monstruos furiosos en un galopar desenfrenado que pareció espantar a las decenas de ratas que caían de nuestros cuerpos.

Ahora todas las noches las observo desde mi rincón oscuro. Las veo chapotear y rabiar unas sobre las otras. Las oigo zumbarse unas maldiciones milenarias. Hasta gracia me han causado. He aprendido a dormir despierto, a nadar en el silencio del alcantarillado, a oler comida en el vacío de la nada. A percibir con mis pequeños ojitos la llegada en la oscuridad de la otra manada.

BUENOS DÍAS COMENSAL

Todos los días llegaba allí para desayunar. La parada, una caja de cristal futurística le servía de comedor público entre los once esperantes que se apretujaban para esperar el autobús. Se acomodaba discretamente entre los usuarios asegurándose de que todo ojo fuera a caer sobre su persona. De no haber el espacio estratégico se sentaba en el suelo y mirándonos de frente comenzaba el ritual del comensal. Depositaba su mirada en cada uno de nosotros, fijándose atentamente en cualquier contorsión facial que confesara un desagrado. Con sumo cuidado, pelaba su plátano maduro, lo depositaba a su lado y luego abría con lentitud felina su lata de comida genérica para gatos.

Cada día resultaba de un sabor distinto, pero los lunes siempre se deleitaba en la de atún, los miércoles en la de pollo y los viernes en la de la variedad mixta. El olor recalcitrante permeaba el cubículo de espera y todo el espacio se volvía de una peste hedionda que sólo se aminoraba cuando algún viento frío nos socorría o alguna que otra señora sacaba su frasco de perfume, disimulando que era hora de retocarse con su fragancia predilecta. En ocasiones contadas ya algún usuario fumaba antes de su llegada permitiendo que los vahos se difuminaran un tanto. Esto irritaba su Karma de sobremanera, ya que chocaba con el ritual de su costumbre matutina.

Primero olfateaba los humos de la carne molida como animal que intenta asegurarse de lo que come. Era un tipo de degustación carnívora, un saborearse el aire antes de meterle el diente a lo gustoso de la carne. Luego de bien olidos los vapores, se bebía el jugo con tal succión que la ponderación de los sonidos llegaba a la parada de enfrente donde los futuros pasajeros paraban los oídos-radares para enterarse del estruendo. Ahora su dedo meñique se encargaría del resto. Afilaba éste despuntado cualquier posible filo de uña que quedase, chupándoselo bien, limpiando todo residuo restante de la uña, cosa que el dedito quedara como limpia cucharilla humana. Escarbaba pequeñas porciones que iban directamente a la lengua donde continuaba la catación y exacto conocimiento de lo que comía. Se relamía en su gusto y de vez en cuando sonreía a sus espectadores mostrando su boca mellada cubierta de gránulos que rehusaban disolverse. En ese momento se atragantaba un pedazo del plátano pasado de su madurez para bajar lo restante de la comida felina.

Aquel deleite culinario se cerraba con una pesquisa detallada del latón de basura cercano, su paraíso de víveres gratis, a ver que se hallaba: una lata de refrescos a medio terminar—a bajarla se ha dicho, una bolsa con dos papitas—a ver si siguen crujientes, servilletas poco usadas para después, colillas de cigarrillos que un humazo se le habrá de sacar, latas, latas y más latas, una cucaracha, unas abejas pero ya no pican, hormigas . . . hormigas . . . hormigas, envolturas plásticas, botellas, periódicos—la sección de buen hogar siempre resulta interesante, latas y más latas y al fondo divisa algo. ¿Qué es esto? El pequeño milagro del día, una lata de atún apenas comenzada—y de las marcas finas. La envuelve cuidadosamente en una de las envolturas plásticas y con la sonrisa más amplia del mundo se despide de nosotros con sus buenos días y un hasta mañana.

DESFILE PUERTORRIQUEÑO

Estimados radioescuchas, televidentes y demás dignos transeúntes de este magno desfile puertorriqueño, les anuncio yo, Pepe de la Gran Peña, su muy agradecido y bien visto locutor, que ha cesado la lluvia y se ve un rayito de sol. Después de todo queridísimo y atento público habrá desfile boricua en esta hermosisisísima ciudad de los rascacielos. Gracias oh gran omnipotente pater rey de los cielos por haber cerrado las puertas del congojo celestial. Parece que se despeja el firmamento y se inicia este magnánimo desfile nada más y nada menos que con el himno nacional norteamericano, tocado por la banda de la Roberto Clemente High School, Atenas del saber bilingüe puertorrisense de nuestra amada ciudad. Con que ejecución y tempo se va melodiando el canto épico de la nación que nos ha protegido en los buenos y en los malos tiempos, ahora Clemente High lo toca con vasto orgullo y marchan con una solemnidad admirable.

Cuanta belleza puertorriqueña va desfilando por estas plateadas calles citadinas, aquí ante nosotros, la prensa, los jueces y demás bien encumbrados, la reina Miss Clemente High se pasea luciendo el último modelo del destacado diseñador Osvaldo de las Pesas. Qué majestuosa, elegantísima, va empapada por la lluvia, pero ella enmutada, como si nada, tanto galbo señoras y señores, les digo que somos toda nobleza, toda nobleza.

—Mira mano, esa jeba me la eché en el mueve que te mueve del bembé de anoche, oye bro cómo me la gocé.

—Dicen que iba más embalá que un cohete sin freno por aquello del spanish fly y el spanish viene.

—Ni papa se le entendía por la maría y por la juana, que si el pae tenía tres pesos y conexión política, que por eso desfilaba. Yo acá no me como ese cuento.

—Mírala como va de trepá, ni te echa el ojo, como si no te hubiera conocido.

—Ay mamita, quien te ve, quien te conoce . . . ayer era otro tu reino.

Seguida y no en menos jerarquía monárquica va la Señorita Rumbera del Sabor bailando nuestra inconfundible salsa que ya ha alcanzado los ámbitos internacionales del ritmo. ¿Dónde no se escucha la salsa? París, Munich, Estocolmo, Barcelona, Tokio, sí señores hasta en japonés nos tocan la clave. Observen la delicadeza, el contorno con que se mueve la cadera para aquí y para allá y todo esto auspiciado por JEWEL FOOD STORES el super de los latinos donde podrá usted encontrar las mejores carnes para el deleite apetitoso del buen diente de su marido.

> Qué bonita bandera, qué bonita bandera,
> qué bonita bandera eh la bandera pueltorrriqueña,
> ma bonita sería, ma bonita sería,
> ma bonita sería si aquí no la escupieran.

—Ya te lo venía diciendo yo que a esta gente no se le puede sacar en público, mira aquél como se seca los mocos con la bandera. ¡Qué asco! ¡Qué horror!

—Qué bonita bandera, qué bonita bandera

—Que te digo que esto es el colmo de la indecencia, mira como aquella tipa se seca sus partes más íntimas y púdicas con lo que queda de la bandera. ¡Qué asco! ¡Qué horror!

Qué bonita bandera, qué bonita bandera,
qué bonita bandera eh la bandera pueltorrriqueña.

Y todo el pueblo se viste de su bandera, la tricolor, la solitaria, la inmaculada, viva Puerto Rico señores y este hermosísimo lienzo que lleva nuestra suprema insignia como pueblo valeroso y luchador de todos los tiempos. Vivan nuestras Miss Universos, una, dos y tres que con tesón llevaron su belleza y la de su pueblo en esta tela representativa de la nación boricua.

—Tanta bandera mano, que chévere, que jolgorio y tú que no querías ni venir.

—No joda, mira como aquel tipo la lleva en la parte de atrás de los calzones, y aquel otro pintá en los calzoncillos.

—Ese otro parece que lleva frío porque va to arropao con ella.

—Guachéate ese cojonú que hasta la cara se la pintó y la estrella la lleva en la mismita sopladera.

—Gringa chula, kiss me i'm puerto rican, que felicidad, mamita no te me vayas así con la trompa alzá, i'm all yours, todito tuyo, puertorican for one day.

¡Qué regio esplendor queridísima y respetada teleaudiencia! La ciudad se colma de alegría para recibir las auténticas bellezas de la isla del encanto. Desde el histórico Castillo San Felipe del Morro nos saludan las tres princesas con sus inigualables y cautivantes sonrisas.

Van representadas las muy nobles ciudades costeras: en rojo rubí encandecente la siempre apasionada ciudad de San Juan, en un vaporoso chifón dorado la perlísima ciudad de Ponce y completando el arca de preciosidades, la magna y sultana ciudad del oeste, Mayagüez en su lame plateado salpicado de pequeños brillantes.

—Ay coño, como me duelen los pies de tanto estar parada y todo esto para complacer a papi; porque si no, no me dan el Ferrari.

—Sonríete nena sonríete, que para eso pagamos un dineral, para treparte allá arriba en tu palacio de cristal, para que esta inculta plebe sepa que ya somos más de acá que de allá.

—Detesto este horrible castillo de cartón, ¿a quién se le ocurre montar este increíble adefesio y tener que sonreír como si realmente me gustara estar subida acá arriba?

—Sonríete amiga sonríe, que somos la total belleza de verdad, mira como estos jíbaros se quedan boquiabiertos, ¿no te encanta? Somos lo mejor de Colgate, Palmolive y Fresh Star.

—Somos toda nobleza, ya lo repitió el locutor, sonríe amiga sonríe, finge que eso nos viene fácil.

Y ante todo amables espectadores—ser bilingüe. Sí mi querido público, hay que tener completo dominio de esas dos grandes lenguas que son el inglés y el español. Esto nos habrá de llevar al progreso, a la dicha y a esa paz que tanto deseamos. EL INGLÉS ES YOUR FUTURE y como bien lo anuncia la carroza de los educadores puertorriqueños con su inmensa estatua de la libertad portando un libro que lee STUDY ENGLISH TODAY BE HAPPY TOMORROW. Les cuento que nada, nada como deleitarse bien en dos lenguas.

—¿Completastes la aplicación del board que tanto te excitaba?

—Fíjate no me dieron el chanse y que porque no sabía hablar o espeliar bueno la idioma. Jasta me dejeron que no conocía bien la populación studiantil de esa zona. Dispués que me quemé las pestañas cuatro anos en el college.

—Yo creo que la problema fue que no tuvistes naiden que te puchara para esa posición.

—No, si yo hice mi networking, si hasta lonché con el mister mandamás.

—Don't you worry, le doy un ringazo y a pichar se ha dicho.

Y a que puertorriqueño no le gusta su buena cerveza, especialmente si es una Bud Light, la cerveza de los latinos en los estados unidos. La orgullosa auspiciadora de las becas para nuestros futuros intelectuales y científicos, como Bud no hay otra igual. En sus fiestas, bautizos, bodas, aniversarios, compromisos, quinceañeras, confirmaciones, comuniones, reuniones, graduaciones, cumpleaños, parrandas, asaltos, viernes sociales, excurciones, día de la raza, de la constitución, día de la independencia, del estado libre asociado, día de los presidentes, de la secretaria, de los maestros, y hoy en el gran día del desfile de Puerto Rico—no le puede faltar la fría—que le recuerda que siempre es hora de gozar, y gozar y gozar más.

—Oye que te hago el cuento del borrachito que veía visiones después de la cuarta bud lite . . .

—Suelta, para ver si me lo conozco.

—Un borrachito que va caminando por la parada puertorriqueña se encuentra un gargajo en el suelo y dice—"¡ay Dios mío pero que medallón de oro más bonito!"—y cuando va a cogerlo . . . dice lleno de sorpresa,—"¡ay mira si hasta una cadena tiene!"

—Mira que lo de vulgar no se te quita, a ver si con esos policías que vienen por allí se te mete la decencia encima aunque sea de ratito.

En este lucido desfile no podían faltar la policía puertorriqueña ni el cuerpo de bomberos boricuas. Ellos presentes en las enredadas, amotinamientos, confrontaciones callejeras, desavenencias domésticas, tiroteos, y demás crímenes menores donde suelen hacer despliegue de su sofisticado entrenamiento, pero no es que esto ocurra mucho en la comunidad, por el contrario, contadas son las veces, porque no habremos de hablar de cosas negativas en este desfile. Porque sí señores y señoras y damitas presentes—hay nobles policías y bomberos boricuas aquí en los United States of America. ¡Qué orgullo para la patria! Miren señores como nuestros bomberos vienen bailando la plena, miren como tocan esa conga, ¡qué cosa más grande!

—Ay papi a que no me apagas el fuego.

Cuando las mujeres
cucan a los hombres
muestran mucha teta
y se las meten
por los cojones

—Ay papi que vulgar, si yo lo que quiero es que me apagues el fuego y me esposes así . . . suavecito.

Desesperá, Desesperá
¿qué será de esa mujer
cuando llegue el pingazal?

*Dentro de nuestra bien civilizada comunidad reina la armonía financiera donde el dólar no falta y los sustanciosos cheques siempre están a la vista. Claro gracias a la Colonial Mortgage Banker que ante nosotros se presentan en su comitiva de Club Puerto Rican Chamber of Commerce, distinguidos y honrados compatriotas de los mejores negocios que se enorgullecen en decirles—***AQUÍ SÍ, AQUÍ SÍ LES ACEPTAMOS LOS CUPONES.**

—Ay mija si no fuera por los cupones estaría yo bien jodía, con cinco bocas que alimentar y ese marido mío que es un mandulete que no da ni un tajo aunque lo maten.

—Oye chica tú no sabe lo que daría yo por regresarme a la isla, pero tú te conoce el refrán, Puerto Rico me encanta pero el welfare me aguanta.

—Pero la verdad que tú eres bien zángana, para que regresar a la isla si la cosa está peor allá, que si el crimen, la droga, el sida, el desempleo, la sequía, las inundaciones, los tapones, la corrupción, las gangas, la contaminación . . . ¡Hay, ni loca! ¿Tú no lees El Vocero? . . . pero que inculta eres.

—Ay bendito pero no hay nada como la patria mija: las playas, las montañas, la gente, la comida . . .

—Las playas están contaminadas, sucias y llenas de petróleo, las montañas eliminadas para construir carreteras y urbanizaciones y eso de la gente, está todita encerrada y ni se le ven los pelos por aquello del crimen, burra te digo que leas El Vocero, ilústrate amiga.

¡Mis colegas, mis colegas! Sí señores aquí desfilan ante ustedes los diferentes canales televisivos y la comitiva es presidida nada menos que por los reporteros de su canal 44, el canal de la

hispanidad, el canal de la felicidad. Porque en las noticias todo es felicidad en nuestro bello Puerto Rico: próxima convención internacional de alcaldes, la nueva Miss Universo, recién aumentos de los salarios gubernamentales, Miss PR Internacional gana en Estocolmo, una estadidad que casi nos viene segura, más programas eróticos para la TV. ¡Qué felicidad para la patria señores! ¡Qué bien nos han puesto el nombre—Puerto Rico! ¿Y qué es esto que ven mis ojos? Es la milicia boricua señores, son los militares puertorriqueños, uniformes, uniformes, uniformes, que gallardos, que guapos, nada como la piel boricua en uniforme norteamericano y nos cuidan hasta aquí en los estados unidos, muy bien que marchan nuestros muchachos, uniformes, uniformes, uniformes.

Un desfile no es un desfile queridísima teleaudiencia sin sus máximos representantes al gobierno federal—y con que orgullo les presentamos en este espectacular e histórico día al primer senador puertorriqueño en Casa Blanca, del Valle our first senator in White House, graduado en derecho de Harvard University, nacido y criado en el barrio, todo un ejemplo del American Dream, aquí para ustedes, porque ustedes lo pidieron y por él votaron, nuestro triunfante del Valle, del Valle, del Valle our great American senator, aplausos, aplausos, aplausos, sí por supuesto . . . Pongámonos de pie ante esta insigne figura de la política puertorriqueña.

—¿Cómo se me ve la corbata?

—Te ves regio, impecable como siempre, pero sonríete un poco más y saluda aquella gente de la tarima que son empresarios.

—¿Me hiciste la cita con el peluquero y el sastre?

—Todo listo, te ponen nuevo mañana, nuevo look—nueva imagen. A ver si los votantes empiezan a olvidarse del affair que tuviste con Alfonso, en mala hora te lo presenté. Te tomamos unas fotos con María Luisa y los niños y santo remedio. El público tiene la memoria de un mosquito.

—¿Me escribieron el discurso?

—Listo. Pasado mañana el barrio completo estará llorando tu pasado y los infortunios de tu niñez y al final completamos con unas promesitas por aquello del plan económico y el favorcito que te debe el presidente. Sonríe, sonríe virilmente, que ahí vienen las cámaras.

Un campeón seguido por otro campeón. Pero éste da los puñetazos en el cuadrilátero. ¡Qué corpulencia! ¡Qué músculos! ¡Qué finura y fuerza de torso! Nuestro Billy Carrasquillo campeón peso pluma, pero el puñetazo se siente de hierro. Mírenlo como boxea solo, es todo un performance piece, a ver . . . ¿y qué nos muestra Billy? Ah . . . es un teléfono para recordarnos que es hora de comunicarnos con A. T. and E, el puente entre las dos culturas. Comuníquense, comuníquense, comuníquense con la isla del encanto, con la mamá, el papá, el abuelo, los nietos, ese ser querido, porque hay tanto de que hablar señoras y señores y damitas presentes que A. T. and E les brinda ese 50% de descuento para que hablen todo lo que quieran, ya no tienen que ir a puerto rico porque existe su amigo A. T. and E. Hablen señoras, porque hay tanto de que hablar . . .

—Oye ayer hablé con mami por teléfono y parece que la cosa está que arde.

—¿Y qué te cuenta?

—A Mari la cogieron en Bayamón oliendo pega, pero lo peor fue que ya venía pegándoselos al marido por aquello de mantener el vicio y diz que se ha metido a puta, pero yo no sé, sólo cuento lo que me dicen porque cuando la cogieron iba más embollá y a la hermana la emborujaron en el lío, no sé si la vendía o la distribuía, el caso fue que también la agarró la jara, pero que pujilato se formó cuando se enteraron de que hasta el hermano maricón que tienen también se la estaba metiendo, ahora dicen que tiene sida, yo no sé, yo te cuento porque la cosa está bien caliente.

Este desfile no puede terminar sin que se coman unos ricos McDonalds porque el Big Mac les dice WELCOME A COMER HAMBURGUERS, WELCOME PORTORIQUENOS A SU HAMBURGUESA PREFERIDA QUE SIEMPRE VA MUY BIEN ACOMPAÑADA DE UNA SABROSA PEPSI, YA SABEN IT'S THE PEPSI GENERATION y quién mejor puede ilustrar esto que el muy charro mexicano que viene cabalgando en su yegua montuna mientras sostiene su gran y burbujeante bebida y a los vientos enarbola nuestra bandera de estrella solitaria, pues viva Puerto Rico no más, ándele pues que no hay nada más importante en la vida que ser Generation Pepsi y eso sí es vivir y lo demás es un cuento.

Estimado público este magno evento cierra nada menos que con un payaso, que buen toque de originalidad y gran sentido de humor por parte del comité organizador. Señores, ¡un payaso! ¡Qué delicia! ¡Qué encanto! Y vestido de bandera de puerto rico. ¡qué gracia, comiquísimo! La estrella la lleva plasmada en la nariz, las franjas rojas y blancas se confunden en dimensiones de multicolor, ¿dónde empieza cada cual?

—Oye, si ese es mi pana . . . que hasta anoche estuvo en la nevera por violar a su hermanita.

—¿Te acuerdas que se hizo el tatuaje de la bandera en las nalgas?

Ahora son miles y miles de banderas que siguen en marcha detrás del divino payaso, miles de banderas estimadísimo público arropando los suelos de esta nuestra segunda patria ¿qué oigo a lo lejos? . . . El güiro suena, retumban las congas, la salsa se ha apoderado del desfile.

—No joda brother, viva pueltorrrico mano, mañana mismo me voy a Borinquen . . . viva pueltorrrico.

Aquí todo es jolgorio y felicidad en este apoteósico cierre, les digo que el New York Times nos dará la mejor reseña nuevamente, aquí fue todo lo mejor de lo nuestro, ¡cuánta belleza, cuánta cultura, cuánta nación, cuánto despliegue, señores! ¡Señores!

DESGRACIA ROMÁNTICA

Entró con su melena deshecha. Parecía que el huracán le había bailado por dentro. Refunfuñaba porque había esperado cinco minutos para el maldito autobús que siempre se atrasaba a la hora más importante de su vida. Fueron cinco minutos de angustia y para el colmo de sus males—sin el cambio correcto que necesitaba para abordar el vehículo de su desgracia. Siempre se le olvidaba recoger aquellos setenta centavos de la cómoda comprada por su abuela en el pulguero de segunda. ¿Cómo era posible que le volviera a suceder esto si cada vez que miraba el mueble heredado se acordaba del regateo de su abuela con el vendedor agitado? Desde entonces se había resuelto asociar el mueble heredado con dinero contado minuciosamente.

Subió al autobús dando tumbos. De repente sintió que toda la gordura se le venía encima. No había manera de que pudiese pasar entre toda esa gente. Le faltaba el aire. Sus axilas se habían vuelto un lapachero de esencias telúricas salpicadas de una fragancia casi apagada. Su frente le sudaba como nunca. Las gotas del sudor le pesaban como plomo muerto que nace, cae y se estanca. El maquillaje se corría y los tonos rosados ya empezaban a confundirse con los bermejos. El sudor se volvía ríos zanjando canales sobre su base Chanel que tanto le había costado. Mala idea fue la de apretarse un poco más la faja esa mañana. Todo por la estúpida vanidad. Le dolían los rollos y comenzaba a sentir el dolor de espaldas que podía fácilmente paralizarla.

La maldición de los tv dinners cobraba su venganza. Cuando se tragó aquella primera suculenta telecena ya conocía los lindes del desempleo. Muy bien le explicó la sicóloga invitada al programa de las cuatro, "que comía por impulso, por ese deseo de apagar toda frustración sexual no consumada debida a todas las otras frustraciones causadas por sus padres que al final de cuenta eran los causantes de su inmensa gordura. Que tenía una necesidad de llenar un vacío, un inmenso vacío que ninguna comida podría llenar jamás." Tal explicación, tan bien pensada, por tan increíble erudita, le pareció una iluminación mística que forjaría el comienzo de su nueva vida.

Viva la tele y sus milagros. Tendría que sondar todos los canales televisivos hasta encontrar la solución perfecta, pero mientras tanto había que comer. De ahí que su doble rollo no le permitiera vivir en sueños de revista MADEMOISELLE. La doble llanta que asustaba a todos los posibles Romeos anunciados por PEPSI tu nueva generación. Mientras tanto iba al trote con toda la inmensidad de su cuerpo que no le permitía el cupo en el infernal autobús de verano. La desgracia se acrecentó con el idiota de chofer que le gritó varias veces,

—Señorota, pague su tarifa.

—¿Quién tiene cambio?

—Señora le aceptan el billete.

—¡Qué no! Qué me gané este peso bien ganao, dando trapos a pisos asquerosos de ricos muertos de hambre. ¿Quién tiene cambio? ¿Aquí nadie come, ni bebe? ¿Dónde está el cambio que le dieron en la tienda?

—Tenga señora, quédese con esto.

—¡Qué no! Qué no quiero limosna, que pa' eso trabajo de sol a sol. Pero, ya que usted insiste . . .

Vio bajar los setenta centavos iluminados por la luz interior del tragamonedas. Aquello le parecía desperdicio que una máquina se comiera lo comible,—Con esos setenta centavos me hubiera comprao un tv dinner de los nuevos que están poniendo a prueba.

La montaña mayor había sido escalada. Todo era cuestión de encontrar un asiento con ventana que le ventilara los sobacos y de una vez ver la ruta de sus planes. Se dio a la empresa de traspasar los precipicios en el aire que sentía cada vez que el chofer caía en uno de los hoyos de la carretera. Todo parecía que los buscaba adrede para verla nadar en el aire. Flotaba y saltaba como astronauta inflada en peripecia atlética. La meta fue lograda con honores conferidos por el público presente que le vociferaba.

—Rema que vas llegando.

—Nada, ballena, nada.

—Acá te espera el cielo.

—¡Virgen Santa que ya estás aquí!

El asiento tan deseado le esperaba con los graffitis más poéticos de la década: AQUÍ TE QUISE CHULA, DÁMELO QUE ES MÍO, A PEDRO YA SE LO COMÍ, PAL CARAJO AL QUE LEA ESTO. Llegó, pero sus nalgas bien extendidas no lograban acomodarse en el aposento de la sensualidad letrada. Por más que trataba se quedaba una porción carnosa colgada en los horizontes perdidos de la nada. Respiró profundamente con la inmensa alegría de saber que había llegado al cielo prometido.

Ahora era cuestión de avalentonarse y abrir conversación con aquél que tan galantemente había ofrecido la tarifa. Notó que desde el comienzo de la odisea había mirado con interés o quién sabe curiosidad a su persona. Ya le había explicado la sicóloga que sí, en efecto eran muchos los hombres interesados en las gorditas. Aquélla sería su tarde de suerte. Le suplicó a San Antonio que le diera tacto y feminidad.

—Y . . . usted ¿qué hace?—preguntó mientras agarraba su enorme bolsa plástica colmada de cajitas de comida pre-preparadas.

—Escribo, señora.

—¿Y vive de eso?

—Me parece que no.

—Decídase, que no voy a estar en este infernal autobús toda la vida. Aprovéchese que me tiene de cerquita ahora.

Ya comenzada la conversación se decidió lanzarse al aventurón del atrevimiento. Nada tenía que perder, tal vez el desagrado de un escritor muerto de hambre. Comenzó con el suave roce de su multidimencional muslo. No, el pobrecito no recibía las señales del erotismo, parecía que iba navegando por los ensueños del escribir. Pasó a la segunda táctica, meter su pie entre los de él. Nada. Él no se daba por aludido. Ya cansada de rozar y meter pierna se acordó que aquello poco valía comparado con lo que se había propuesto antes de tomar el autobús. En cuestión de minutos llegaría al almacén de su dicha.

Llegó a su destino: a la tienda de la constante barata. COMPRE HOY—PAGUE MAÑANA, COMPRE UNO—LLÉVESE OTRO GRATIS, AQUÍ LE FINANCIAMOS, AQUÍ SÍ LE QUEREMOS, AQUÍ LE DAMOS TODO LO QUE USTED QUIERE. La sonrisa se dibujó en su rostro mientras daba comienzo al final de su travesía. Intentó varias veces alcanzar el cordón para pedir parada, pero sólo logró perder el balance y desequilibrar la nalga aérea. "Oiga, ¿por qué no me alcanza y Dios se lo paga?" El letrado accedió a esta última petición. Esperó a que el autobús parara en seco para comenzar el descenso de la alegría colmada. Iba inflada de esperanza con pie seguro a conquistar descuentos y descubrir especiales que solamente ella podría encontrar. Su salida fue triunfal, llena de dimes y te dirés,—de cuanto te odio y yo te odio más.

NOCHE DE RONDA

Me miro ante el espejo y descubro un rostro que no conozco. ¿Cómo fue posible que toda esa elaborada belleza haya desaparecido en el transcurso de una noche? Con espanto crítico se revelan ante mí unas ojeras azules y profundas que enmarcan estos ojos de pájaro azorado. El fino delineador, el rimel, la sombra azul, todo se ha vuelto un charco de colores oscuros, donde apenas se asoman unos ojitos lagrimosos cubiertos de venecillas rojas a punto de estallar. El labio inferior, descolorido y seco, me tiembla con la rapidez de aquél que sufre escalofríos en invierno. Trato de morderlo para apaciguar el llanto, pero en vano el intento, porque el sollozo se revienta en mi boca, dando alaridos que no puedo contener.

En esta desesperante angustia, quiero agarrarme de los cabellos y tirar de ellos hasta sangrar, pero me desenmascaro con la verdad de que la frondosa cabellera de anoche es ahora una peluca entre mis manos y la prematura calvicie muestra estas cejas despintadas, donde el sudor ha surcado canales que llegan hasta las mejillas hinchadas. ¿Cómo es posible este esperpento, si anoche fui la envidia de las amigas, el centro de todos los cumplidos? Y ahora heme aquí, más atropellada que víctima de incendio, terremoto, huracán o todo combinado, adolorida, arrastrada hasta este infernal espejo donde arreglo cuentas conmigo misma, con la vida, donde veo esta cara que rehúso mirar y me niego a sentir este cuerpo tajado de cicatrices recientes, golpeado y apaleado como si la muerte lo esperase a la vuelta de la esquina.

¿Dónde estoy yo, Maritza la siempre bella, la perfumada, la dueña de la esquina y la noche? Te busco en este maldito espejo y no te encuentro, te desmaquillo y no estás ahí, sólo veo este espantapájaros de ser, esta sombra de sombras que no es Maritza de la noche. Y voy urdiendo en la memoria hasta recordar el mundo que construí, esa verdad que habíamos creado para poder sobrevivir.

Todo comenzaba con el régimen de nuestra estética, aquello que nos hacía bellas, espléndidas, listas para la nocturna ronda. A la hora de ponernos el maquillaje siempre nos divertíamos mucho la Lucy y yo. Ella más negra que la noche, le daba con pintarse con afeites de niña blanca, de tonos rosados como si fuera de quinceañera. Yo lógico, le recriminaba que se dejara de complejos, que íbamos a putear, no a desfilar en Casa España. Ella se hacía la tonta y continuaba sombreándose con su pink translucent eyeshadow. Se colocaba todas las cremas y polvos con el delicado esmero de una cosmetóloga profesional mientras cantaba rancheras a lo Rocío Durcal. Después de una ardua hora frente al espejo, quedaba yo regia, como para levantar el primer macho que se me cruzara en el camino. Pero no, me tenía que revestir de paciencia y remover la falsa máscara blanca de Lucy para transformarla en una diosa africana. Ella sí que era toda una mujer. En cuestión de minutos y con poco maquillaje se vislumbraba la diferencia inmediatamente.

—Condená, tú sí que naciste para ser mujer. Con esa carita de ángel y ese cuerpo de guitarra no hay mujer que se te pare al lado. Papá Dios se equivocó solamente en el pipí. Y ahora que tu raza está de moda . . . no joda.

—Ay querida, pero si el color no me ayuda . . .

—No seas pendeja. ¿Para qué tú quieres ser blanca? A ver . . . Si las blancas nos arrugamos más rápido que una pasa y a la primera enfermedad que nos da, parece que nos llevó la muerte. Tu tranquila con la cuestión del color, que tú siempre eres la primera en hacer el levante, conque tranquila, ¿ok?

Aquellos vestidos que vimos en **ELLE** y que luego nosotras mismas confeccionamos resultaron perfectos. Mi querida Lucy, siempre soñaste con vestir de vampiresa inocente y aquel conjunto negro se ceñía a tu esbelto cuerpo de guitarra como una segunda piel. Qué clase, qué estilo tenías al caminar. Bien que parecías un cisne flotando en un lago tranquilo de algún país exótico. Esa blusa transparente marcaba hermosamente los senos que habíamos diseñado. La falda tomaba las curvas de tus levantadas nalgas, para mostrar unas caderas que gritaban que querían ser acariciadas.

Yo, en cambio, la desgraciada, no había nacido con la bendición de tu cuerpo. Mi estructura ósea masculina me delataba a leguas, por lo tanto había que camuflarlo con mucha tela suelta, cosa que el enfoque quedara siempre dirigido a mi obra de arte, a esta cara de mujer pintada con el más diestro pincel.

Cada ceja que nos dibujábamos, cada prenda que vestíamos nos acercaba más al sexo tan admirado. Nuestras voces cambiaban, la dicción se nos tornaba perfecta y los manerismos femeninos surgían con una naturalidad que ningún hombre se podía resistir a ellos. Nos mirábamos al espejo y sin lugar a dudas quedábamos convencidas de que éramos mujeres. Tú la exquisita modelo de revista y yo la impactante mujer de cosméticos.

El taxista que nos recogió en la esquina no quitaba la mirada del retrovisor. Te comía con los ojos y tú tan distante como siempre, conocedora de que poseías la belleza que embrujaba los hombres, no te dignabas en echarle ni siquiera un ojito. Él se mojaba los labios, se los mordía, suspiraba, todo esto sin que se registrara en tu mirada de diosa intocable. Al bajarnos rehusó aceptar el pago por el uso, en ese preciso momento como estratagema bien planeada, le soplaste un beso al aire, que el muy pendejo recibió como si fuera enviado por el cielo.

—¿Qué carajo tú les haces a los hombres, amiga?

—Nada niña. Les brindo mucho silencio, misterio y creo la ilusión, la fantasía de que existo bella, pero no soy de ellos.

—Y si te descubren . . .

—Los hombres son unos pendejos y se les engaña fácilmente.

Cuando entramos al club la música estaba encendida. El son cubano se había apoderado del ambiente para darle al lugar un toque extravagantemente tropical. Estaban las caderas que no se podían contener. El roce suave de los cuerpos incitaba al baile, al cachondeo. Se bailaba el baile de la losa sencilla. Cuatro piernas bien entrenzadas se movían despacito dentro del pequeño espacio cuadrado. La flauta y las maracas marcaban la clave, mientras el güiro raspaba el aire. Sudaban las pieles soltando unas fragancias de perfumes bien cotizados, se cuajaba el pre-aroma del sexo tamizado por el buen oler. El agua ardiente se hacía sentir en las carcajadas, en los labios mojados que regalaban besos por doquier. El lugar no era para aplatanarse, aquí se vivía la intensidad del momento. El desesperante deseo de manifestarse en cuerpo y alma era la orden del día. Y tú tranquila, como si no estuvieras incluida en la lujuria de la noche, como si aquello no pasara por tu lado.

El guapetón de Mario te echó el ojo desde que hicimos la entrada. El muy zorro hacía un par de meses que te venía tirando el lazo y tú tan indiferente como siempre. Sus ojos azules dormilones enloquecían a las competidoras, las pobres suspiraban como tontas adolescentes al verlo pasar. El condenado sabía como acariciarse el cabello rubio ondulado, dar la media vuelta, flexionar los músculos y seguir la pasarela exhibiendo su traje italiano al estilo Armani. Todo ese despliegue para su Lucy. El pobrecito empeñado en su diosa africana, que le diría cosas tan dulces como—guaca-naraya guateque guateso, ay amor te voy sintiendo ya la o—. Pero todo esto te colmaba de tal aburrimiento que hasta en la cara se te veía el deseo de salir corriendo. Aquí no se daba el juego que tú querías. El adivina, adivínalo más, para ver si sabes con quién te acostarás.

—Ya vámonos que estoy harta de estar aquí.

—Pero chica, ¿qué te pasa si apenas llegamos?

—Esto me aburre mujer, acá todos saben lo que somos. No hay intriga ni misterio. Estos son unos semi-machos que se quieren comer el cuento de que se acuestan con una mujer, pero saben muy bien que tenemos el coso que nos delata. En este lugar no se ha seducido a nadie. Vámonos a conocer los hombres de verdad, los que realmente se crean esta fantasía que hemos elaborado. Ya después que prueben un poco, no dan marcha atrás.

Siempre terminábamos en esto, tu juego, tu deseo de querer ser aceptada por lo que en el fondo no eras y pretendías serlo. Porque ya te habías creído el cambio y vivías en otro cuerpo, en esa fantasía de la fisonomía creada. Y yo como siempre la insegura, la fácil de complacer, la acomplejada, que por ganarme tu estimación te seguía hasta el fondo de la barranca. Hasta hallar el porque de nuestro peregrinaje por la noche.

Nos fuimos del club y comenzamos a ondular caderas. Caminamos seis o siete pasos cuando se detuvo ante nosotras uno de tus admiradores, el taxista, el devorador de tu mirada. El chofer se había conseguido un amigo que no estaba del todo mal y ahora nos invitaban a subir al carro. Aquello para ti era fantasía mayor, hacer el amor con un taxista que te acortejaba como si fueras mujer irresistible. Lógico que ya te venía esperando, el tipo había leído bien la señal que le diste cuando le lanzaste aquel beso aéreo que esperaba su llegada y ahora aterrizaba aquí en tu mirada. Esta gente no come cuento, te dicen exactamente lo que piensan, sin tapujos, sin la menor consideración de que se están dirigiendo a unas damas.

—Mamita chula, preciosa, ¿damos un paseo por el parque? Mira que la noche está como para chupárselas todas. No me ponga esa cara de ofendida y aquí el que sufre soy yo, porque huelo canela, pero no como canela.

—Por lo visto Maritza el taxista tiene lengua y habla, porque en el taxi no dijo ni pío.

—No sólo tengo lengua, sino que la sé usar como a ti te gusta mi reina.

—Y tú, ¿qué sabes lo que me gusta a mí?

—A ver, súbete mi belleza y lo descubro.

El hombre dio en el clavo cuando dijo la palabra descubro, porque precisamente ese era tu mundo cubrir y descubrir para agradar con la sorpresa o aterrorizarse con la verdad. Seguir con tu juego, ese era el plan, porque en todo caso la vida era jugarse las cartas y en eso resultábamos expertas. El deseo de subirte al auto se notó de inmediato. Comenzaste a frotar la manija delicadamente como tentando la idea, hasta que por fin tiraste de ella y nos subimos al coche. El taxista se conocía a perfección la zona y en menos de media hora estábamos en uno de los parques más remotos de la ciudad. Allí todo era oscuridad y de un silencio que espantaba muertos. Estacionó el auto entre los arbustos y casi al unísono, los dos se lanzaron sobre nosotras con un apetito devorador.

Harto nos conocíamos el cuento, querían ir directamente al epicentro de la acción, a la ranura del deleite femenino, pero eso nos delataría, pondría fin a nuestro secreto juego. Para aquél entonces, ya hacían tres meses que veníamos inyectándonos las hormonas, por lo tanto muchos eran los placeres que podríamos brindar antes de descubrir el secreto. El plan siempre era el mismo, dirigirlos lentamente por el camino del eros, paso a paso, hasta culminar en la entrega total, si era aceptada. Los largos y profundos besos, las apasionadas caricias, eran el preámbulo que los llevaría a chupar con fuerza los delicados senos.

El taxista y su compañero se acoplaron al momento, se dejaron llevar por nuestras diestras manos que los guiaban como ciegos, ya la prisa no existía, pero el calor iba en aumento. Poco a poco nos desvestían mientras mordían, besaban, apretaban todo aquel cuerpo que se les entregaba femeninamente. Noté que Lucy se apresuraba, que algo la sacaba del camino estudiado. Su acompañante se le alteraba, colocaba con tesón su miembro erecto entre las piernas de mi amiga, exigía prontitud en el acto. Ella para socorrerse del momento, se arrodilló ante él, sacó su enorme e incandescente hierro y comenzó a mamarlo para apaciguar la demanda de su taxista.

La situación comenzó a empeorar. Mientras el taxista se dejaba complacer, noté como con insistencia buscaba la vulva de Lucy y ella se esquivaba, le buscaba la vuelta para que él no diera con lo que él tanto apetecía. Esa noche mi amiga se había forrado herméticamente su carga de hombre con cinta adhesiva. Llevaba su ínfimo bulto masculino apretado entre las piernas, casi aplastado contra su piel, de manera que al tocar por esa región sólo se podía sentir si acaso una leve protuberancia.

Lucy no contó con la fuerza inesperada que de repente mostró su hombre. En cuestión de segundos le echó una llave y seguidamente le abrió las piernas con la invasión de las suyas. Al quedar completamente expuesta, buscó con desesperación la apertura que tanto se le negaba. Cuando palpó con su enorme pene el pequeño paquete adherido a la piel de su vencida, el rostro le cambió de expresión, se consternó la mirada y con una fuerza brutal tiró de la cinta exponiendo al aire los genitales colgantes de mi amiga.

Sin darle tiempo a que ella se preparara, comenzó a darle puñetazos en la cara, a sacarle sangre por los ojos y la boca mientras le gritaba sin parar, "maricón de mierda, ésta me la pagas con tu vida." Después que se cansó de pegarle, sacó de la guantera un cuchillo y con la misma rabia renovada le enterró el puñal en el pecho repetidas veces hasta sacarle su último grito de vida. Todo esto ocurrió como un relámpago. Yo había quedado paralizada, inmóvil, sin saber que hacer ante aquel horror inesperado.

Todavía quedaba yo, y el amigo se sentía obligado de mostrar su machismo y camaradería con el cuate deshonrado. Me susurró al oído, "no me cuesta más remedio nene"—y esto me lo decía porque nosotros nos habíamos sentido, él sabía muy bien en lo que se había metido y estaba dispuesto a seguir hasta lo último si no hubiese sido por la desaprobación de su amigo. Había que probarse, era la ley de la vida. Sacó de su bolsillo una manopla y comenzaron los golpes dirigidos al vientre que lentamente iban subiendo hasta llegar a mi cara, como tortura lenta de que había que deformar aquello que tan fácilmente lo sedujo. En sus ojos se le notaba una tristeza que no iba a la par con la paliza que vaciaba en mi cuerpo. Lo nuestro había sido distinto. En el silencio de las caricias habíamos develado nuestras verdades, el gusto por lo que él conocía prohibido, pero no obstante gustaba de ello. Mis gritos y llantos, la sangre derramada, ayudaron a convencer al taxista de la hombría de su amigo.

—Estos hay que dejarlos tirados en carretera abierta para que el tráfico termine con ellos—propuso el taxista.

—Mejor a éste lo dejamos aquí para que no se levante la sospecha.

Me miro en este espejo y aún puedo ver los coches pasando sobre tu cuerpo. Vacía de toda vida los parachoques te lanzaban de un lado a otro de la carretera como bola desinflada, sin el menor indicio de detenerse para recoger el bagazo humano que rodaba por el asfalto. Cuando me recuperé del desmayo, ya tu cadáver había desaparecido, no sé si por el tanto rodar o por algún alma que se apiadó de aquel horrible espectáculo.

Intento quitarme este maquillaje que se ha incrustado en mis heridas, pero sólo logro causar más dolor a esta piel ya deformada. Este infernal espejo es el asesino de mi alma que me sigue recordando la deformación de mi rostro, del recuerdo de una belleza inventada. Te voy buscando en este reflejo mi querida Lucy, pero las coordenadas de tus ojos se me escapan y sólo logro escuchar esta caja ruidosa que me anuncia tu muerte, tu descalabro por la vida,—"homosexual travesti muere atropellado por un auto"—es todo lo que se oye. Me miro en este espejo para traspasar esta nada que no veo y quedo fragmentada, rota en mil pedazos, buscando los restos para construir tu mirada.

EL ENJAMBRE

Este afán de volverse uno de enredarse en las sábanas de buscar la entrada al placer de conseguir el dominio del éxtasis en una sola palabra de multiplicarse en las sílabas del sudor acentuando la dejadez del cuerpo que se nos muere en cada salida sin el tiempo de llegar al perdón porque el perdonar no existe en este acto de amor que no es amor siendo el más allá del placer que se tritura en cada pedazo de piel en cada boca que se nutre de su propio sabor aumentando el calor de cada suspiro de cada quejido de cada gemido de gozo en la embriaguez de eso que nombran líbido liviandad para sentirse entregado a toda agonía a cada mal paso tomado porque tomarse el aire del otro es vivirse-vivir en esto que nominan la fuerza del cuerpo que quiere sentir lo que se sabe que se desconoce en la sangre que se acumula en el vaso que se extiende fortaleciendo cada vena cada vía de todo ese tránsito forzado sin escape a lo lejano que queda tan cerca tan apretado tan amarrado a sí mismo que pide liberación invitando al beso extraño al beso que pulula entre la suavidad del tacto y la ruptura abrupta de esa pequeñez deseada y negada porque no se niega se pospone todo lo que se desea de esa locura cuerda que electrifica los sentidos confunde el intelecto y arrastra hasta el no más amor porque es que deseo más allá de lo que conozco porque en cada pedido se descubre que nunca se ha comenzado este círculo de los brazos entregados y extendidos a esa tu fuerza de querer llegar de querer depositar todo el desenfreno que ya no puedes acumular porque te has liberado has visto que este afán de volverse uno es multiplicarse.

CUENTO PARA SER CANTADO

el prefigurado

Sueles hacer tus visitas de mañana cuando los pájaros aún cantan, cuando el café se aroma en el viento y hermosamente estás recostado así, desnudo, entregado con todas las fuerzas viriles al aire como imponiendo un cerco de felicidad, de una dicha que sólo tú conoces, Prefigurado, cuando haces visitas de mañana y tomas tu tiempo teorizando el amor en cada roce, en cada palpitación de mi cuerpo que es tu cuerpo en invención, porque bien sabemos que no existes, que solitario llegas con tus huellas a imprimir en lo profundo, a dejar tu sabor a piel, a pájaros que aún cantan en la noche.

inicio

Sé cuando me miras con tus ojos verdes de verano, que la piel se te va quemando, tejiéndose en un atavío de bronce. Y bien tu piel, fuerza de músculos apretados que asonantados van persiguiendo esta oscura mirada antillana que se te cuela por los ojos, por ese verde mar que llamas mirada. Y conocerte en una noche de fuego cuando los latones de Jamaica tumban y retumban los sones de calipso y limbo, es descifrar el enigma que te hace hombre, imaginarse el salitre del sudor que permea tu cuerpo, hoy día del encuentro, de las primicias, de saberse iniciado en el amor, ¿cómo saber que eres tú, el Prefigurado, el hombre que ha de ser el hombre?

angela's cafe

Aquí está por nacer nuestro amor. Éste tu primer sorbo de café, los labios acercándose a la taza como anticipando el beso. Nos miramos con un miedo de siglos, porque los hombres no han de quererse con la intensidad y el descaro que nos queremos. Hacemos una trenza con las palabras que nos definen, descubriendo que en cada vuelo se ha encontrado al otro. Tu sonrisa se filtra por mis poros y vuelvo a sentir esa mirada de verde mar. ¿Adónde me llevas con tus claros ojos? ¿Cuál es el cabotaje de tu piel? ¿Cómo se descifra la primera cita de recuerdos? Nos palpamos las manos debajo de la mesa, revelando el secreto, descubriendo la mentira, porque los hombres no se habrán de amar así, con el descaro que nos amamos.

los paseos

Las pisadas nos van llevando a estos manglares hermosos donde los caimanes se ocultan bajo las sombras de un árbol. Sigilosos descienden a sus aguas oscuras donde sus vértebras se asoman por un breve momento. Así vas descubriendo mis primeros miedos, los temores de un caribeño que jamás ha visto lagartos de enorme tamaño. Me dices que has nadado en sus aguas, que es cuestión de acostumbrarse a la idea, de que todo es lo mismo, animal, agua, vida y muerte. Admiro ese sentido extraño del valor, un entregarse a lo que es ya uno. Niño que es hombre. Hombre que es niño. La tarde se va abriendo, salitrada, perezosa de ánimo. Hemos llegado al palmeral, a estas arenas que nos unen desde mi isla a tu península. A lo lejos, el horizonte langostino nos traga con su boca naranja, ampliándose desde sus entrañas para mostrar el monstruo de garras azules pintadas. Y nos vamos imaginando en este trueque de atardeceres, cómo es tocarse las manos, sentirlas palpables, táctiles, llenas de una fuerza incontenible donde se deposita el deseo del amor censurado. Porque el afecto no será público, sino en los lindes de la imaginación, donde lo silente siempre permanece vociferado de amor. Aquí las hojas se amontonan a nuestro paso. Explorándolas descubrimos un tiempo que no es nuestro, algo diluido por los minutos que van pasando, horas imprecisas, horas estancadas. Los paseos me llevaron a conocer tu vida, un laberinto de luces que ha cercado el aire, el viento que define la existencia.

TABLE OF CONTENTS/INDICE

A MATTER OF MEN

CUESTIÓN DE HOMBRES

BIOGRAPHIES

BENITO PASTORIZA IYODO

Benito Pastoriza Iyodo is an award-winning author from Puerto Rico. He has received various prizes in the genres of poetry and short story. The Ateneo Puertorriqueño awarded him prizes for his book of poetry ***Gotas verdes para la ciudad*** *(Green Drops for the City)* and the short story entitled *El indiscreto encanto (The Indiscreet Charm)*. He received the Chicano Latino Literary Prize for his book of poetry entitled ***Lo coloro de lo incoloro*** *(The Color of the Colorless)*, published by the University of California. His works have also won prizes in literary competitions in Australia and Mexico. His collection of poems, ***Cartas a la sombra de tu piel*** *(Letters to the Shadow of Your Love)*, earned the prize Voces Selectas. Pastoriza was cofounder of magazines specializing in the diffusion of literature written by Latinos in the United States. The first edition of his book of short stories, ***Cuestión de hombres*** *(A Matter of Men)*, was published by The Latino Press (CUNY). His books of poetry, ***Cartas a la sombra de tu piel*** (2002) and ***Elegías de septiembre*** *(September Elegies)* (2003) were published by Editorial Tierra Firme in Mexico City. His second book of narratives, ***Nena, nena de mi corazón*** *(Beloved, Beloved of My Heart)*, was published by Xlibris in December of 2006. His novel, ***El agua del paraíso*** *(The Waters* *of Paradise)* was released in April 2008 by Xlibris. Currently the author collaborates with academic and literary magazines in the United States, which have published his interviews of distinguished poets, essays and book reviews. His writings have been published in the magazines: **En Rojo, Línea Plural, Taller Literario, Cupey, Luz en Arte y Literatura, Los Perdedores, Mystralight, Vagamundos, Carpeta de Poesía Luz, Hofstra Hispanic Review, Visible** and **Literal**. His poetry also appears in the U.S. anthology ***Poetic voices without borders*** and in Terra Austral of Australia. His works have been published in Australia, Mexico, Chile, Spain, Puerto Rico and the United States.

BRADLEY WARREN DAVIS

The translator's first encounter with Spanish and its culture was at the young age of 14 when he went to Colombia as part of a "sister city" exchange program. His fascination with the language and culture was immediate. At that time he did not yet speak any Spanish, but using gestures and dictionaries he took his first steps in learning to communicate with his hosts. His Colombian experience included travel to various cities, which permitted him to observe and participate in some of the traditions of the country: their dances, music and festivals.

His second encounter with Spanish took place at Davidson College where he earned his liberal arts degree in sociology and anthropology. There he embraced the study of Spanish language, culture and literature. In his sophomore year he studied in Spain where he took courses conducted in Spanish regarding sociology, Spanish theater and Spanish civilization. In Spain he also had the opportunity to travel through Andalusia, Valencia, Castile and Extremadura.

During his law school years at the University of Miami, he served as the interpreter for a group of Florida citrus specialists on a fact-finding mission to Cuba. This experience included interaction with Cuban governmental officials that accompanied the group as it traveled the island. Davis interpreted for these officials as well.

Since then Davis has incorporated Spanish into his professional life: as a bilingual attorney; as a curriculum and bilingual materials developer and as a translator and interpreter for both Hispanic and U.S. firms. He has also participated in translation symposia. His translations have been published in newspapers, literary publications and magazines including **Arte en Luz y Literatura**, **Visible** and **Literal**. His experience as a translator and interpreter has been enriched by numerous journeys to Latin America, including: Puerto Rico, the Dominican Republic, Mexico, Costa Rica, Honduras, Guatemala, Ecuador and Venezuela. Presently he has several translation projects in process that will be published soon.